Sweet Marmalade Abbey

A Comforting Tale from Detroit

Joseph N. Mazzara

Publishing Coordinator – Sharon Kizziah-Holmes
Cover Design – Jaycee DeLorenzo

Paperback-Press
an imprint of A & S Publishing
A & S Holmes, Inc.

ISBN -13: 978-1-956806-04-5

DEDICATION

This book is dedicated to the good people of America who seek comfort and sanity in a world that is seemingly lacking in both.

ACKNOWLEDGEMENTS

Special thanks are due to John and Lisa Dane who provided excellent editing suggestions and gentle nudges to fix all the parts that needed fixing. Nearly fifty years of friendship and a mutual appreciation for the genius of Kurt Vonnegut, Jr. has bound us together almost into one mind. Finally, last, but certainly not least, I want to thank my loving wife, Cindy, for her unending support and encouragement throughout this project. When Cindy said "I don't think so…" I listened.

INTRODUCTION

I wrote this book during the Covid-19 pandemic. At the time, many people had already died of the infection and even more feared for their own health and safety. As if this were not enough, the country was being roiled by violent protests in our cities, and in the capitol of our country.

The rift between left and right, intensified by the media, pitted black vs. white, minority vs. minority and religious vs. secular Americans. The divide had never been more pronounced. A sitting president was impeached, and the subsequent election was challenged as being corrupt.

Anger and fear were the defining emotions of our time. Civility was in short supply. This is so sad. America, I thought, was in dire need of some peace, comfort and hope.

I decided I would write a book in which most of the characters are kind and gentle, and all of the characters would have some dignity and value as human beings. I wanted the book to be a comfort to the reader and an affirmation of the enduring value that Judeo-Christian culture has given to Western Civilization.

The title came to me before the story: Sweet Marmalade Abbey. It would be about a quirky but lovable group of Benedictine monks living in an inner-city monastery. They would face their own struggles in faith, and in relating to the ever-changing outside world. Although the monks are Catholic, I believe that everyone, regardless of race, religion or political persuasion can take comfort in the monks' emulation of Christ in their daily lives.

Love, gratefulness, forgiveness and humility are key ingredients in the monks' profound sense of contentment, much in contrast to the prevailing culture of our times, where power, hatred, victimhood and revenge are the currency of the day.

The book does not preach. Rather, it shows by example that there is another way to live, a way in which we can love others as we love ourselves. Oh, yeah…it will also make you laugh.

JM

CHAPTER 1

Something nefarious was afoot in the neo-gothic oratory of the St. Adelaide Abbey. While several monks solemnly observed the celebration of a matins service, one monk stood in the shadows on the far-left side of the nave. Concealed behind a massive stone pillar, Br. Philip paid little attention to the sacred hymns and readings of his brothers. He was, instead, focused on finding the means and opportunity to carry out his attack. The timing would need to be right and his target unaware of what was to happen.

The interior of the room shimmered in reflection from the candles that danced and played in the darkness of the walls. Familiar fragrant spirits arose from the incense, as if working the room to greet each monk with the welcome presence of an old friend.

It was two o'clock AM, a time known to the monks as "Why, in God's name, am I up at this hour?" Br. Philip, a slender monk in his late twenties, scanned the somnambulant wave of bobbing heads and drowsy eyes that were his brothers at prayer. It was, he thought, an ungodly hour for anyone other than a monk to be awake. He wished that he could doze off too, into some grand lucid dream of REM escape. Maybe he would sail without wings off the peak of Mt. Everest, onto a graceful landing in the soft grasslands of Nepal. Or perhaps he'd have a sordid romance with the prettiest nun from the nearby Sisters of Mercy convent. There would surely be no moral repercussions because, as all monks know, you can't be held responsible for your actions in a dream. Dreams are nature's perfect get-out-of-hell-free card.

Br. Philip was getting bored. Why was he not more engaged, he wondered? Maybe he wasn't cut out to be a monk. At that point, he was brought back to the world by the pleasant, sweet-sounding chant of *"Lord, you shall open my lips and my mouth shall declare your praise."*

Toward the front of the sanctuary, Br. Canisius, older than Br. Philip, and one of the more sincere and pious monks, was singing. He was clearly enraptured by the solemnity and harmonious beauty of the moment. Has modern music, he wondered, really improved from the Gregorian chant? But alas, such single-mindedness came at a cost. Br. Canisius was, at that very moment, seriously lacking in situational awareness. One could not, it seems, be focused on both the spiritual and corporeal realms at the same time. The singing stopped, leaving, only the sound of crickets chirping. Br. Philip waited and watched Br. Canisius closely. He tracked him with an eagle's eye until he decided that it was the time to spring. He conveyed himself, as quiet as a cat burglar, three rows forward to the empty pew behind Br. Canisius. He sat and waited for his chance. Sensing his best opportunity, Br. Philip dipped his bony finger into the small blob of sticky orange marmalade he had secreted in the sleeve of his black robe. He inched his finger, bit by bit, ever closer to the target: Br. Canisius' left ear lobe. At just the right moment, he pounced. "Psst, brother," he whispered.

Br. Canisius reflexively turned his head, thereby jamming his ear into a sticky morsel of past its sell-by-date marmalade. He turned immediately to face his grinning tormenter.

"Knock it off, idiot," Br. Canisius mumbled sotto voce. "This is matins. Act your age and have some respect for the Lord."

"Hey, lighten up Canisius," said Br. Philip, "you had a sour look on your face so I just tried to sweeten it up a bit."

Now Br. Philip was hit with a distinct but well-deserved pinprick of remorse, if not actual guilt. Strangely, not for the harmless prank played on Br. Canisius, but for his most un-monk-like lustful thoughts about those innocent Sisters of Mercy. Poor ladies, he thought, Lord forgive me. He said two quick Hail Mary's as a preemptive penance. He would soon need to say more than that.

CHAPTER 2

The Abbey of St. Adelaide was a small stone mini-fortress in inner-city Detroit. Within the sacred compound were several stone and granite buildings including the oratory, a refectory, a large commercial kitchen and the old chapter house, now used as a counseling center for the local residents. The center was funded through charitable donations and profits from the monks' primary business, the baking and sale of marmalade tarts so delicious that St. Adelaide Abbey was more commonly known locally as Sweet Marmalade Abbey.

It was not an ancient edifice. Built in 1898, it was a mere child compared to the great cathedrals of Europe. There were no flying buttresses, but the monks took pride in its clean stone and marble floors as well as its foot-thick granite walls. Within walking distance, were other relics of the Motor City: Woodward Avenue, the first paved road in America, and the historic Piquette factory where Henry Ford built the first Model T and developed his ideas for applying the assembly line concept to automobile production. There was no soup kitchen at St. Adelaide, in contrast to their more famous cross-town counterpart, St. Bonaventure Monastery, the onetime home of Blessed Solanus Casey, a Capuchin monk on his sure way to sainthood – with a bullet.

Solanus Casey was a humble man from Wisconsin who came to Detroit's St. Bonaventure in hopes of becoming a priest. As it turned out, he lacked the academic skills necessary to become a full priest. Instead, he was ordained as a "simplex" priest, one who was not allowed to give sermons or hear confessions. Unfazed, the meek priest served as the doorkeeper to the church where he also started a soup kitchen to feed the needy. He became the most beloved priest in Detroit and was said to have contributed to myriad miracles through his intercessions to the Lord. Even at St. Adelaide Abbey he remained an inspiration to all of the monks.

There were twelve monks with varying levels of commitment and/or piety living at the Benedictine abbey. The Abbot, Fr. Albert, was a harmless eighty-five-year-old man of Italian descent. His face showed ample evidence of age, but his aquiline nose and great shock of silver hair softened the damage, giving him a somewhat handsome appearance. When he took his vows, he chose the name Albert in honor of St. Albert of Trapani, the birthplace of his Sicilian parents. Ironically, his pre-monastic surname was actually Costello, a detail not lost on those monks who still retained a sense of humor (this would not include Br. Canisius). In the minds of his charges, Fr. Albert would forever (but secretly) be known as the Abbot Costello. The gentle abbot helmed the venerable ship with a steady hand, while simultaneously holding the private conviction that all was lost. The two-thousand-year primacy of Judeo-Christian values in Western culture had, in Fr. Albert's view, been rusted through like the fender of a 1965 Plymouth Valiant. It had been almost completely destroyed by modern day do-it-yourself morality and bespoke ethics. No amount of Bondo, thought the old cleric, could disguise the rot. In Fr. Albert's view, traditional faith was based on the simple premise: *"This is what the church teaches, and this is the truth."* In more recent times that sentiment had given way to the more egocentric *"This is what I personally believe at this moment."* Fr. Albert did not think that Western Civilization would ever survive this level of solipsism.

At breakfast after the mass, Br. Philip found Br. Canisius and apologized for the prank. "Don't worry about it. Philip," said Br. Canisius, "I forgive you. I just hope that Jesus will too."

Br. Philip hoped that there would be no hard feelings between them.

After Fr. Albert said grace, the men sat in silent prayer as they ate a hale breakfast of farm fresh eggs, thick-cut bacon, homemade sourdough bread and, of course aromatic marmalade tarts. Orange, today. The monks always ate well in return for long hours of work, prayer and contemplation. Despite the ample food, few of the brothers were overweight, save for the chief cook Br. Manuel. Br. Manuel was rotund. He had a puffy brown face punctuated only by shiny coal-like eyes, a thin moustache and a smile that announced his love for everyone he met. Br. Manuel came from the vibrant and historic Hispanic area of Southwest Detroit. Once a member of the *Bagley Boys* street gang, he had been "born again" during the Jesus Freak movement of the 1970s and became an evangelical Christian. As he got older, he felt a calling to return to the church of his ancestors and his youth. He once again became a Roman Catholic, entered the Abbey of St. Adelaide and chose his monastic name in honor of St. Manuel Gonzales Garcia who shared the surnames of his mother and father.

Br. Manuel had one peculiar attribute that endeared him to his brothers but also spooked them. Br. Manuel had a sensory disorder known as synesthesia. Somewhere in his brain, his olfactory neurons were crossed in such a way that specific odors or scents were experienced by him as sounds. Some smells elicited pleasant sounds, others grated like fingernails on a chalkboard. The scent of lemon marmalade made him hear dice clicking over a wooden tabletop. Orange marmalade on the other hand, evoked the sound of angels singing. Given his position as head cook, he heard this aroma a lot. Diesel exhaust from city busses sounded to Br. Manuel like the music of Iggy Pop and The

Stooges. There were other aromas for which Br. Manuel would not disclose what he heard. It made for a most curious kitchen experience.

Late to the meal was Br. Bede who joined the group with a terse apology. "Sorry," he said.

Br. Philip nudged Br. Canisius and whispered, "Good thing we got here before Br. Bede, there might have been nothing left."

True, Br. Bede was an imposing man, six-foot five at least, with muscles that refused to atrophy even after years in the monastery, but it would not be like him to eat more than his share. He was the proverbial gentle giant in size, humility and love for others. He sat down gently and smiled to no one in particular. Monastic life had given him the face of contentment.

"Good to the last drop." The words were muttered by the elfin little brother sitting next to Br. Philip. At ninety-six years of age, Fr. Berthold was the oldest man at St. Adelaide. His cognitive faculties long diminished, he now spoke using mostly old advertising slogans or taglines. Some of his utterings seemed appropriate to the subject, but most were complete non-sequiturs. Occasionally the other brothers would discern real meaning from his strange pronouncements. Once, at a funeral for a young oblate that had died of cancer, Fr. Berthold was rumored to say "Goodbye brother." Those who actually heard him were quite impressed until he followed it up with "Don't leave home without it." Many of the brothers wondered how much time the old man had left.

CHAPTER 3

Fr. Albert waved his hand in a general circle to get everyone's attention. "I need some volunteers," he said. "First a couple of you need to make a bread-run to the Avalon today. Second, someone needs to welcome the new therapist to the counseling center. Her name is Sarah Kessler and she'll be here tomorrow at 9:00 AM."

The Avalon Bakery supplied all the bread for the monastery. In earlier days the monks baked their own bread, but since the marmalade tarts took on a life of their own, the monks no longer had the time to bake both bread *and* tarts. Avalon International Breads, as it is formally known, opened about twenty-five years ago in what was then known as the Cass Corridor. At its nadir, the infamous Corridor was primarily home to prostitutes, drug dealers, junkies and the largest collection of down-on-their-luck homeless souls in the city of Detroit.

Avalon quickly became the go-to destination for rich organic breads and other delicious home-grown baked goods. It also served as an early catalyst for the near miraculous rejuvenation of the neighborhood now gentrified and rebranded as Midtown. The brothers of St. Adelaide loved the artisanal breads and willingly made the brief two-mile trek down Woodward Avenue as often as needed.

"We'll do the bread run," said Br. Philip, answering for Br. Canisius as well as himself. Br. Canisius didn't object to being drafted for the job as, pranks notwithstanding, he and Br. Philip often liked to get out and see the city.

Br. Bede volunteered to do the orientation for the new therapist. He held a Ph.D. in Clinical Psychology from the University of Detroit Mercy and also served part time as a therapist at the Guidance Center. Other therapists at the center generally felt safer when Br. Bede was working. There was no security guard and the presence of the big monk was reassuring.

After breakfast, the monks readied themselves for the day ahead. In the kitchen, brothers jostled about with trays of all the finest flour, sugar and fruits most suitable for tarts. Although orange marmalade was by far the best seller, they also employed alchemy to transform apples, limes, nectarines and Traverse City cherries into gold as the spirit moved them. The sweet redolent presence of so much delicious fruit mixing with the intoxicating aroma of butter melting into the dough baking in the brick ovens, was enough to gratify even the most unyielding of olfactory receptors. Br. Manuel described the kitchen experience as that of hearing Stravinsky's *Rite of Spring* for the first time.

Brs. Philip and Canisius helped out in the kitchen until the first batch of tarts was dislodged from the oven. It was March, but still cold, so they drove rather than walked a load of tarts over to the Avalon where they would trade them for a few days' worth of bread. In warmer weather they would sometimes walk the route pulling a small wagon. Today, they loaded the sweet goods into the back of their 2004 Pontiac Aztek which they Christened the Tartmobile.

Br. Philip, also known as "the car guy" by fellow monks for his broad knowledge of vehicles – good and bad, smiled and said to Br. Canisius, "You know, I am always humbled when we drive this car through the streets of Detroit. It was surely the most hideous looking car ever produced in America and to add insult to injury, it was painted in the brightest yellow that General Motors could invent, as if to ensure that drivers could not hide from the stricken stares of passers-by. I should be embarrassed but instead, I gladly accept this as a lesson in humility."

Br. Canisius, being the safer driver, took the wheel and they motored south down Woodward Avenue. Br. Philip observed the cityscape and made trenchant remarks about the denizens of Detroit. A homeless man ambled down Woodward with a full measure of used pop and beer cans in his cart.

"Hey Canisius," he remarked, "There, but for the grace of God go you!"

Br. Canisius ignored the snarky remark.

Br. Canisius parked in the No-Parking zone in front of the bakery, knowing that they would not likely be there long enough to attract the attention of Detroit's finest. If they were caught by the Parking Enforcement officers, they knew that forgiveness could likely be obtained through the simple indulgence of a free tart.

Inside the bakery, they were greeted by Carla, everyone's favorite cashier, whose genuine hundred watt smile could burn a hole into the center ice at Little Caesar's Arena.

"Hey my monkity brothas," she said, "I got y'all's bread packed up and ready to go. Now gimme those tarts before somebody buys them all and I'm left sniffin' crumbs."

Brs. Philip and Canisius always enjoyed the small amount of time they got to spend with Carla. Br. Canisius once told Br. Philip that this is what Jesus meant when he said that we should be good witnesses for the Lord. "Spend a minute with that woman," he said, "and you know that she has something that does not come from this Earth."

"We should all be that happy about our faith," mumbled Br. Philip.

"So true," Br. Canisius replied. Then, after a pause, "But *are* you?" he asked. "Really. I just mean that, well lately, you don't seem yourself. Your singing at mass is half-assed and your weekly prank ratio is almost down to zero. I don't mean to pry, but if there is anything you need to talk about,

I'm your brother, man. In both senses of the word."

"I'm alright," snapped Br. Philip.

Br. Canisius let it drop. Both men played their gender roles perfectly. Had this been two women, the first one would not likely have accepted a simple "I'm alright." She would have first gently encouraged and then mercilessly badgered her sister to spill the beans. The hectored woman would then have caved, and without too much effort from the first woman. This is the thing about men and women. Women bond through relationships and the expression of feelings where men bond through things. Maybe Br. Philip, "the car guy" would have opened up more readily had Br. Canisius asked him if he thought that a Dodge Challenger Hellcat could beat a Shelby Mustang GT 500 in the quarter-mile.

The brothers returned to the abbey and helped once again with kitchen chores until vespers. In a Catholic abbey or monastery, every member of the order knows with certainty what comes next. There is no wondering what one will do with the rest of the day. It never changes. All Catholic orders, in one form or another, follow the Rule of St. Benedict, laid down in the sixth century. Also known as the *Liturgy of the Hours*, the *Divine Office* or even the *Opus Dei*, this set of rules governs everything from the schedule of prayers for each day to how the brothers will relate to each other and to the Abbot. Far from being oppressive, the Rules free the members from the normal worries and decisions of the day and provide a structure for them to emulate the way of Christ. In practice, like a train that stays on the track, the Rules bring the monks into closer harmony with the Divine Plan.

Between vespers and compline, the brothers had the scarce treat of some free time. They tried to use this time wisely and productively before succumbing to the sublime pleasure of retiring at night's end. Some prayed in the chapel, some in their cells. Others read books or engaged in hobbies like crafts or music. Br. Canisius lost himself in an article about the relationship between Flannery O'Connor and the Trappist monk Thomas Merton. Br. Bede sat on his bed quietly thwacking his ukulele. Br. Manuel was devouring every page of a new cookbook of recipes from Downton Abbey. Br. Philip rested on his bed staring up at the ceiling and listening to the slow peal of St. Adelaide's church bells.

CHAPTER 4

Br. Bede was first to the refectory the next morning, just after the completion of Lauds. He loved the morning prayers as they set the tone for the day. He hung his head downward and said a short prayer of praise and gratefulness. Praise for everything God has created and a humble spirit of thanksgiving for all that the Lord has done for him personally.

Like Br. Manuel, Br. Bede was the product of a less than optimal upbringing. Mother died of a drug overdose when he was ten years old. Dad was an alcoholic who tried his best to raise the family, using the only parenting style he knew – authoritarian with physical punishment as a back-up.

Br. Bede had two younger sisters and one younger brother. All of them reaped the benefit of

Br. Bede running interference on their behalf, especially when the blows were physical. In his teens, he took up boxing and weightlifting, dropped out of school at seventeen and lived on the streets for a while. Later, he worked as a bouncer at several clubs, including the strip club on Eight Mile Road where he almost killed a man who, after being ejected for rowdiness, returned to the club with a gun. Br. Bede quit the bouncing business that night, eventually converted to Catholicism, and now enjoyed the comforting structure and rhythm of monastery life.

Br. Philip came in and sat down next to Br. Bede. "Hey," he grinned, "isn't today the day you are supposed to meet the new therapist? I heard she's a real looker."

Br. Bede sighed and shut his eyes. "Brother Philip," he said, "did you forget that you are a monk? You should have learned to tame your lust long ago. Sarah Kessler, as I understand it, is a fine young woman and a well-regarded therapist. Her physical appearance is irrelevant."

"I'm sorry," said Br. Philip, "you're right. I don't know why I still act like an adolescent sometimes."

Br. Philip's contrition was real. He knew that of all the brothers at St. Adelaide Abbey, he was probably, no definitely, the most immature. Shortly after arriving at the abbey he was caught hiding a dog-eared copy of *Portnoy's Complaint* under his mattress as if it were pornography, which of course it was. Lately, he had been acting out his inappropriate thoughts in silly ways. There was the marmalade incident on Br. Canisius' earlobe and just before that he was reprimanded for referring to a brother who suffered mild epileptic attacks as "Sid Seizure."

"It's as if I have no filter between my brain and my mouth. Do you think that I might have an underdeveloped prefrontal cortex?"

"Yes," said Br. Bede.

After breakfast, Br. Bede made his way over to the Guidance Center next door. He was warmed by the early sunshine as he walked across the cracked asphalt of the parking lot. Imagine that, he thought, the day has just begun and I have already received gifts of warmth and light. "Life is good," he shouted out loud.

The St. Adelaide Community Guidance Center served the local residents who could not afford to see a private therapist and did not want to linger on the long waiting lists for outpatient treatment at the underfunded Detroit/Wayne County Community Mental Health Service centers. Therapists at the Guidance Center came from all walks of life and many were ex-priests and nuns who had left their religious communities but still wanted to minister to the poor. Others, like Sarah Kessler were fresh out of graduate school with their master's degrees in clinical social work, psychology or counseling. It was a pretty good first job or, for those more established, a good moonlighting gig.

Br. Bede walked up the steps and into the lobby to a waiting passel of souls in need of healing balms. There were no wingback leather chairs or oak paneled walls in this place, only some threadbare chairs and wobbly coffee tables, but somehow it still managed to give comfort.

"Good morning Brother Bede," said Mrs. McNulty, "and how might this fine day find you?"

"I'm great Mrs. M, and ready to slay some monsters and demons. With words of course," he smiled, "not weapons."

"Sure" she said, "it wouldn't be the first time a victory was earned from the jawbone of an ass."

Br. Bede erupted with a belly laugh that resonated through the lobby like a thunderclap. Mrs. McNulty was in her seventies and had the face of a proud Irish matriarch. Elegant, or handsome if you will, her head was always without a stray blue hair, and held high as she had been taught by her parents. She kept a stern visage as a matter of principle, but would break in to a conspiratorial grin as quick as the spirit moved her. She was the longest serving worker at the center and worked in the Guidance Center as well as the abbey office. She used her seniority as a license to humble the haughty whenever she got the chance. Few people could get away with such shenanigans but Mrs. McNulty had that razor-sharp wit and a disarming smile that told you it's all for fun. And fun she was. Except for protocol. She addressed everyone by their title and last name, and expected no less for herself. She was hard core old school in that regard.

Br. Bede looked around the waiting room and saw one person who stood out from the crowd. Young and pretty with a crisp blue business suit and a smile to match, she projected professional confidence rather than despair. Br. Philip was right, allowed Br. Bede, she *is* a looker. The woman's shoulder length auburn hair framed her lovely face like a well-chosen matte around an artist's portrait. A looker indeed. "Ms. Kessler, I presume, I am Brother Bede. Please come in."

The two exchanged pleasantries before moving on to the business of the day. Br. Bede learned that Sarah Kessler was Jewish by family history, but not so much in practice. Her faith was not much deeper than sharing a family Seder with her parents at Passover or a perfunctory menorah at Hanukah. She had a newly minted Master of Social Work degree with a clinical concentration from Wayne State University. She inquired as to whether her faith would be a problem at a Roman Catholic counseling center. Br. Bede smiled and assured her that she had been hired for her clinical skills and not for her religion.

Since this was Ms. Kessler's first day at the clinic, she would be assigned to do an intake evaluation on a new client with follow-up supervision by Br. Bede. Her first client (the term "patient" had been long since retired as too medically biased) was a twenty-two-year-old man who had been arrested at a local demonstration (against all things establishment) that had turned violent. A counter-protestor in her seventies had been knocked to the pavement and the man who did it, one Hunter Stephenson, was arrested. The judge, being sympathetic to the cause, offered Mr. Stephenson the option of counseling instead of jail. Naturally he took it. "I'm not one to look a gift horse in the eyes," he told the judge.

Br. Bede gave Ms. Kessler a little time to review

the chart and said he'd meet with her next week.

In the counseling office, Sarah sat back in her chair and savored the experience of her first professional job. The desk and bookcases appeared to be early big-box modern and the client chair was of similar provenance. It didn't matter. She was now officially a psychotherapist. It's not like this was her first client, but it would be her first paying customer. She sat in silence to fully appreciate the moment. This is awesome, she thought. Her brief reverie was interrupted by the voice of Mrs. McNulty. "Welcome to the clinic, Ms. Kessler," she said, "Mr. Stephenson has arrived."

CHAPTER 5

Sarah walked out to the lobby and introduced herself to the morose young man named Hunter Stephenson. "Hi Mr. Stephenson, my name is Sarah Kessler. Please come in and make yourself comfortable."

Stephenson actually looked quite comfortable already. He had been earnestly slouching in the chair, but got up and walked ahead of Sarah into the therapy office. He was a lanky six-footer with a scruffy beard and a nascent man-bun. His face was nondescript save for the snake tattoo on his upper neck. It might have been a rattler, but it was poorly rendered and bore a closer resemblance to an earthworm. His uniform was standard for the day: a fine pair of ripped jeans, a well-worn pair of *Chuck Taylor* sneakers (in black) and a loose-fitting plaid flannel shirt over a T-shirt bearing the iconic hagiographic image of the celebrated racist murderer known as Che Guevara.

"How can I help you today?" asked Sarah

"OK," he said, "I'll be honest with you right up front. I'm here, because the alternative is going to jail, and, nothing against those dudes, but I'd rather sleep in my own bed."

"I understand, but as long as you are here, is there something I can help you with?" she said with authentic concern.

Hunter thought, but remained silent.

"As long as you have to be here, we could make it as pleasant and productive as possible."

"Or," she said, "if you really don't want to be here, I will respect your wishes. I can call your probation officer or the judge to let them know that it would be a waste of both of our time. I don't want you to be here if you don't want to be, but I'll be happy to work with you. It's your choice and I'll respect whatever decision you make."

"Crap. Why does everyone always put it on me?" he asked. "First my parents, then the judge, and now you."

"It's called responsibility," she replied. Her grin showed that she had him by the short hairs, and Hunter acknowledged as much.

"Alright," he sighed, "then let's get this party started. What do you want to know?"

Sarah gathered the information she needed like a seasoned pro. She always thought that the role of a therapist in the beginning was that of a gentle Torquemada. "Tell me about this…" Tell me about that…" In no time at all, she had gleaned that

Hunter was the son of upper middle-class parents who had divorced just before his freshman year at Birmingham Seaholm High School. His father worked in upper-level accounting for General Motors, and was described by Hunter as "basically an asshole." His mother was a nurse practitioner at nearby Beaumont hospital. Hunter said she was nicer than his dad, but that she always stood up for her husband and not him.

After the divorce, his mother had several "loser" boyfriends but she never remarried. Hunter was the third of five children and true to his birth order, often felt invisible. He had left his parents' home a year ago and moved with some friends into an apartment near Wayne State. He took some political science classes at WSU for about a year, but couldn't get excited about any of them, so he decided to take some time off.

"I'm taking a hiatal from my studies," he informed Sarah.

He could not identify any emotional problems for which he might need help, but did admit to some anger issues. "That's why I was at the demonstration," he said, "when I get pissed off, I feel better if other people are pissed off too."

Sarah Kessler wanted to delve further immediately, but their time was already up and she made an appointment to see Mr. Stephenson again next week.

As he got up to leave, Hunter asked "Are you gonna tell my P.O. that I get pissed off a lot?'

"No, Hunter, everything we talk about is confidential and I can only share it with someone else with your written consent. Or... with a court order."

CHAPTER 6

After the men had finished their breakfast, Fr. Albert wanted to talk business. First was the suggestion that the abbey add a new item to the menu: a Bakewell tart. It seems that Br. Canisius had received a visit this week from his Aunt Veerle who lived in the Dutch city of Utrecht. She had recently vacationed in England and had stopped at a quaint little teahouse in the cathedral town of Salisbury. At the café, she enjoyed the most delicious Bakewell tart that she had ever tasted and brought one home for her nephew to sample. Br. Canisius told Fr. Albert that the tart would make a great addition to the Abby's offerings. The men voted overwhelmingly to add the tart, and Br. Manuel said he would find the best recipe. He could already smell Satie's *Gymnopedie No 1*.

"Thank you, Brother VanOesterhoven, for your

contribution," Fr. Albert said, using Br. Canisius' given surname.

"More like Brother Van Toaster Oven if you ask me," said Br. Philip just a wee bit louder than he intended. As usual, Br. Canisius was not offended, but he was getting a little tired of Br. Philip's shenanigans. Fr. Albert looked directly at Br. Philip; his left eyebrow now arched sharply upward in a manner that Br. Philip correctly read as the dreaded Italian malocchio. He knew there would be repercussions.

Other business included Br. Bede's positive report on the new therapist, Sarah Kessler, a discussion about finances and expenditures, the failing commercial stove in the kitchen, and Fr. Berthold's announcement that he fears a syphilis outbreak in the barracks. Of course, the superannuated Father was no longer allowed to say mass or hear confession.

There was one final comment from Fr. Albert. "Brothers, we are about to begin the hour of Terce. Remember that Jesus appeared to the apostles at that very hour at the Pentecost. So…let's be holy out there." As a big fan of the old television show, *Hill Street Blues*, he loved to end meetings with his own take on the "*Let's be careful out there*" line.

With the business concluded, Fr. Albert dismissed the brothers to begin Terce, and motioned for Br. Philip to join him in his study. Like a dog caught chewing the sofa, Br. Philip hung his head and followed his master down the hallway. The walk of shame, as it was known, was primarily an internal event. Fr. Albert was a kind man and Br.

Philip knew that no real harm would come to him, but still, it was humiliating. He had let himself down. He had been caught once again acting the fool and perhaps proving to himself more than to others that he was not ready for the pious dignity of monastic life. He felt as doomed as a Baptist church bus on a winding mountain road.

The Abbot's private office was comfortable, but not ostentatious. Wood paneled walls framed the carved fireplace of the longest wall. Old leather easy chairs in various parts of the room stood waiting to give comfort to old friends and penitent monks alike. Many paintings and icons brightened the oak walls. Knickknacks were dispersed about the room like disjointed memories. The only items suggesting modernity were a tiny black and white television, and the Abbot's favorite comfort, an original black leather Eames lounge chair that he bought new in 1962.

"Please have a seat, Brother Philip," he said without a hint of irritation or anger.

Br. Philip eased into the chair and before Fr. Albert could speak another word, said "I know why I'm here Father. That crack about Van Toaster Oven was juvenile. I sometimes say things without considering the consequences. I am sorry, and I really do feel bad about my behavior lately."

"Maybe you have an underdeveloped prefrontal cortex," he said. He watched Br. Philip's face turn from puzzled to wounded before he grinned and said "I'm just joking, Philip, it's OK."

Br. Philip returned his face to near normal.

"Here's the thing, Philip, I'm concerned about

you. I am the shepherd of this godforsaken flock and when one of the brothers goes astray, I am troubled. Of course, it's not just the jokes or the teasing, although they alone are evidence that you may not have your thoughts entirely focused on the Lord these days. There are other things. You seem unhappy. Where is your Joy of Christian life? I also notice that you don't sing during masses like you used to. I would welcome hearing that wonderful off-key excuse for a tenor voice rise above the rest once in a while. Tell me Brother Philip, what's wrong?"

Br. Philip didn't answer his interlocutor immediately. He distracted himself with trivial thoughts of his current state. The Rule of Benedict prescribes standards for disciplining wayward monks. The progression always follows the same pattern. It begins at *reprove*, then, if needed, goes to *entreat* and finally *rebuke*. He had been reprimanded several times in the past, so that covered the reprove part. This did not feel like a rebuke, thought Br. Philip, so he must be on second base. This is an entreaty.

"I don't know, Abbot Albert," he said. "You are right, I have been feeling a bit restless and depressed lately, but I don't know why. I thought that I had devoted my life fully to Christ, but now, I am not sure. I miss my family and friends. My mind wanders a lot lately and I find myself thinking about girls, I mean women. Sometimes I wish we had something like the Amish rumspringa where the young people can sow their wild oats and be welcomed back when they are finished."

"Ah," said the Abbot, the old 'I want to go to heaven, but I don't want to die' routine. Unfortunately, we Benedictines don't have a rumspringa. You are expected to commit for life. Anyway, if we did let you go, we would likely have to shun you upon your return. Listen Philip, all Christians occasionally have doubts. We have to push through the doubts to keep our faith strong."

"Do you have doubts Abba?" asked Br. Philip.

Now it was Fr. Albert's turn to be quiet and reflective. After a brief pause, he replied "Yes Philip, I have my own moments of weakness."

"What kind?" asked Br. Philip. "Do you also think of women and long for your old life?"

"No, no, not that," said Fr. Albert. I am old. I have had many years to come to terms with the things I have given up for this life."

"What then? asked Br. Philip, "What do you struggle with?"

CHAPTER 7

Fr. Albert hesitated. Should he share his weakness and doubt with his brother who was yet a subordinate? Or should he mask his own shortcomings, so as to present to Br. Philip a powerful, but false model of the brave and faithful leader? As he pondered this dilemma, the abbot realized that at this very moment he had been given a gift. For years, he had longed for his own confessor, someone who would listen to his concerns and give him guidance. Now an unlikely one had been dropped in his lap. Such were the unappreciated gifts from God. Fr. Albert had for quite some time been laden with the weight of his own doubts but had no one with whom he could confide. Now, in front of him was a flawed man, also in crisis, who was willing to listen. Fr. Albert began to weep. Not a stifled whimper but a chest heaving paroxysm of cathartic release. This went on for more seconds than he would have thought proper. Br. Philip remained silent.

When he regained his composure, Fr. Albert began to empty his soul into the ears of his fledgling brother. "Philip, my friend, I don't know where to start. I have lately begun to doubt whether Catholicism or even Christianity itself can survive the corrosive effects of modern western civilization. I occasionally watch the television news and read the newspapers only to be assaulted with a constant barrage of anti-Christian values. Boy Scouts are bad, transsexuals are saints. Priests are all child molesters but gay men are to be applauded for their courage. Women who abort their babies are to be celebrated while right-to-lifers are portrayed as bigoted nut-jobs. How on earth did we get to this point of backwardness?

"It's as if," he continued, "the current generation is completely untethered. They are untethered from religion, untethered from family, untethered from history, untethered from everything of any lasting value. When I look out of my sheltered monastic window, I don't see Detroit or America, I see a simulacrum of Sodom and Gomorrah."

"I'm sorry to hear this father," Br. Philip said, "I always saw you as our rock, someone who pressed on regardless, through thick and thin, in good times and in bad."

"Philip," said Fr. Albert, "I am a man, no different than yourself. You are tormented by doubts about your worthiness to serve Christ and I am a man tormented by doubts that our struggle is at all worthwhile. In truth, I feel that we are losing the battle. How can we win when our message says that because Christ died for our sins, we must curtail our impulses and desires in order to live a life worthy of the Lord's sacrifice? The other side, and by that, I mean Satan, modern secular culture and the predominant zeitgeist of the twenty-first century, tells people that they alone are responsible for determining right from wrong, they alone decide moral values and anyone who tries to impose values from the outside are bigots, charlatans, fascists or worse. Imposing *our* values? Hah! Isn't it *they* who tell us what words we must use and *they* who tell us that a confused man who believes himself to be a woman is, in that case, accepted without question to be a real, actual woman? Truth is, anyone who is not a moron can see that this new moral framework leads to nowhere but anomie and spiritual death"

Fr. Albert's use of the term anomie almost made Br. Philip giggle, but he didn't. It brought him back to Sociology 101 at the University of Detroit. Émile Durkheim had proposed the idea that the absence of shared and useful norms in a given society resulted in a disconnect and sense of alienation among the lesser connected members of that society. Br. Philip thought that in today's world, the alienated group was most people.

"But Father," Br. Philip began, "wasn't it that way from the beginning? Didn't Christ Himself tell us that 'If the world hates you, realize that it hated me first?"

"Yes Brother Philip, I'm aware of what Christ said."

"Sorry, Father," Philp replied.

"Here's the thing, my young brother," the abbot continued, "from the beginning, his disciples knew that they were going against the grain. They received hatred from day one, but chose to endure it out of faith that Christ was who He said He was, the Son of God. They were very brave. What about us though? After two-thousand years of Christianity, and more than five-thousand years of Judaism, we became Christians at a time when it was more or less the norm. There was nothing scandalous about declaring yourself a Catholic in mid-twentieth century America. Because of that, we took our acceptance for granted. Sure, there were a few atheists and kooks who had an ax to grind, but they were always in the minority. We were welcome then.

"It is not that way now. You're too young to remember, but we used to say daily prayers – in a public school!" The volume of his tremulous voice rose, and at that point Fr. Albert knew he had to stop and think for a minute. He was quickly spooling up into a category five rant and felt in danger of morphing into the proverbial old codger screaming at the children to get off of his lawn.

Br. Philip looked downward. "Can I get you some tea Father?"

"No, no. Thank you, Philip, but I'm OK. I have taken more of your time than I had planned and spent most of it talking about myself. Look, we need to talk again soon, but I'll leave you with this: I don't see you as a lost cause, and I think that you have the capacity to become a fine man of the cloth someday. But in the meantime, please spend some time praying for some more maturity, and I am sure the rest will fall into place naturally. And one more thing. On this morning's bread run, I want you to stay home and pray. Brother Canisius can find another hand among the brothers. You have your own work to do."

As Br. Philip walked away from the Abbot's office, he thought to himself, bingo, I was right. I just received an official entreaty to change my ways. He was, however, also concerned about Fr. Albert's current state. I've never seen the old man so down and dispirited, he thought. He wondered what he could do to help.

CHAPTER 8

Walking back to his room, Br. Philip encountered Br. Canisius coming toward him. "How was your talk with the Abbot Costello?" he asked, hoping that some humor would soften Br. Philip's embarrassment.

"It went fine," replied Br. Philip, "but I can't go with you to the Avalon today." He felt like a grounded teenager telling his friend that he was not allowed to play baseball on this fine, sunny day.

Sorry to hear that," said Br. Canisius, "we'll do it the next time."

Br. Philip went to his room and knelt on the small, padded hassock at the foot of his bed. He said a sincere and sober *Our Father* and a *Hail Mary* before dipping a toe into the waters of contrition. In private, he had no reason to feel embarrassed. In fact, his relationship with God was a comfortable one where he felt no need to hide his feelings or thoughts. He, like other monks and clergy, prayed so often that it was not only second nature, but was central to his being. He felt that when he was in true prayer, he was literally in another place. With God. "Lord," he prayed, "you know me well. What's wrong with me? Am I a whited sepulcher? Sometimes I feel like a floater in the gene pool." He almost thought that he heard the voice of God reply, "Maybe it's an underdeveloped prefrontal cortex," but he knew it was not God's way to joke with a man's salvation.

Even during mass, Br. Philip knew that he was not fully engaged. The hymns and chants were enjoyable enough, but even more, Br. Philip treasured the brief breaks between songs. There, he absorbed the simpler spirituality of silence. There is something about quiet that allows us to turn inward and give access to the everyday sounds that are always there, but normally hidden by human activity. Rather than immerse himself in the mass, Br. Philip would listen to the gentle squeak of Br. Bede's ancient leather brogues as he shifted his weight in the pew. An occasional cough would echo through the room like a perfectly tuned wooden clave. Even the low hum of the HVAC system caught Br. Philip's attention, as it had an ASMR-like calming effect.

Br. Philip prayed in earnest for about an hour.

He prayed for maturity and self-control. He prayed for dominion over his lust, and noticed that the more he prayed, the more his mind wandered over to thoughts of the lovely Sarah Kessler. "Begone Satan," he muttered to the opportunistic one.

His prayer was interrupted by a knock on his door. Upon opening the door, he encountered Fr. Berthold in his underpants holding out a small pack of weathered and yellowed pages. "War bonds," announced the old monk, "buy some."

Br. Philip accepted a few of the worthless papers and gave Fr. Berthold a dollar to keep him happy. "This Bud's for you." said the satisfied brother.

CHAPTER 9

Br. Canisius, had enlisted Br. Bede to help him with the Avalon bread run. Without the usual play by play coming from Br. Philip, the ride down Woodward Avenue in the bright yellow Tartmobile was peaceful. When they arrived at the bakery, there was a commotion going on inside. Carla was yelling and trying to restrain a man who had apparently just stolen the tip jar and several loaves of bread. Br. Bede gently stepped between the two combatants and glared at the man. The thief looked up at the giant monk in the robe and thought with certainty that he was directly facing the grim reaper. He dropped the jar and the bread, and scrambled out the door like a frightened cat. Carla started to chase the man, but Br. Bede told her to let it go. Meanwhile, Br. Canisius and some of the other shoppers were helping to pick up the fallen items from the floor.

"Brother, you got here just in time," said an out-of-breath Carla.

"I don't think that he would have hurt you," said Br. Bede, "he just wanted the money."

"Hurt me?" Carla said with not a little indignation. "He's the one would've been feeling pain."

After Carla had calmed down and the store was put back together, she gave a little grin. "I'm sorry brothers, you know that I'm a Christian lady, but sometimes you got to protect what's yours. Those tips belong to all of the workers here, not just me."

Br. Bede assured her that he would not turn her in to the "Big Guy Upstairs."

"Here," he said "try one of our new Bakewell tarts."

Carla nibbled cautiously on the fresh treat as one would an apple of uncertain ripening. She then broke into a wide smile and chomped into the pastry like a starved woman. "Oh my God," she swooned, "this is your best work yet! Gimme another."

Even the staid Br. Canisius grinned with pride. "I'll give your humble review to Brother Manuel who is the mastermind behind the recipe."

"Oh my God," she said again, and called her co-worker Angela over to confirm her delight. Angela gushed over the tart.

"If you think that is delicious," bragged Br. Bede, "try it sometime with real English clotted cream."

The brothers left the goodies, picked up their

bread and waved goodbye to the women.

"Brother Manuel will be very pleased," said Br. Canisius

CHAPTER 10

Sarah arrived at the clinic early and was surprised to find Hunter Stephenson waiting for her in the lobby. "Hi Hunter," she said, "did you know that our appointment is for two o'clock? You're an hour early."

"I know. Do you mind? I had nowhere to go and I thought that I might just as well hang out here as anywhere."

"You can if you like, but I can't see you until two," she replied.

Sarah said hello to Mrs. McNulty, who gave her a sly wink and said quietly, "You are wise beyond your years, Ms. Kessler."

Sarah's excellent training and Mrs. McNulty's years of experience gave each of them the appreciation for keeping appointment times as they were. Unless the client was in a genuine crisis, you didn't establish a pattern of seeing them on demand. Sarah suspected that with Hunter's background, he was given to manipulation and testing of limits. A young man like Hunter would actually feel safer within a structure set by the therapist, but he would never admit it to himself.

Before the session, Sarah met briefly with Br. Bede for clinical supervision. He brought with him a fresh Bakewell tart for her to sample. "Oh my God, that's good!" she said.

"That's the third time today I heard that reaction," said Br. Bede. "Maybe we should call it the OMG tart."

The two clinicians discussed the first session Sarah had with Hunter Stephenson. They both agreed that he appeared to be an angry young man with a chip on his shoulder, but they didn't yet know why. Sarah told Br. Bede about Hunter arriving an hour early for their session and how she made him wait. "Nice move," said Br. Bede, "you are good."

"Thank you," said Sarah, "but I have a question. Am I assuming too much to think that his parents' divorce might be a contributing factor? He did seem to have a lot of anger toward authority figures, his father in particular."

Br. Bede replied. "Of course, you don't want to assume anything, but I think it's a good place to start. Most children of divorce carry the scars for a long time, big or small. There are a few kids who actually do better after their parents' divorce, but they are the exception and not the norm. Hunter was in middle school when his parents divorced. That's a tough time even without your parents splitting up. I feel sorry for kids these days. The gold standard of an intact family with a mother and father who love each other and their children, is unfortunately rare these days. No wonder the kids don't leave home until fifty and don't get married until they are eligible for social security."

Sarah laughed. "You keep calling them kids. Hunter's only a few years younger than me."

"Yeah," said Br. Bede, "but I doubt that you ever pushed an old lady over at a demonstration."

"You never know," she replied.

On his way out, Mrs. McNulty grabbed the sleeve of Br. Bede's arm and asked, "Where is my Bakewell tart, Brother?"

Br. Bede was caught slightly off-guard but said, "Why Mrs. McNulty, I thought if you got any more tarted up, you'd be risking arrest by the cops."

"Touché," she replied, "but you'd better bring one next time."

Sarah finished up some paperwork and headed out to the lobby to see Hunter Stephenson. He was not there. "Mrs. McNulty," she asked, "have you seen my client Mr. Stephenson?"

"No," she replied, "he was just sitting there a few minutes ago, reading that infernal Rolling Stone magazine. I didn't see him leave."

Sarah looked around the lobby and then asked a male co-worker to check the men's room. Hunter was not there. Great, thought Sarah, my second week on the job and already my first no-show. But it wasn't really a no-show. He was here, and then he wasn't. Why would he wait almost an hour and then leave, she wondered? She waited fifteen minutes for him to return and then wrote a brief note about the incident in his chart.

As Sarah was leaving, Mrs. McNulty tried to give her some comfort. "I wouldn't worry about it," she said, "it happens all the time."

CHAPTER 11

On her way out, Sarah decided to stop by the abbey and tell Br. Bede what had happened. The man who answered the door was Br. Manuel. He knew who she was, but was taken aback because it wasn't often that such a fetching woman crossed the threshold of the abbey. Besides that, Br. Manuel immediately caught a whiff of Sarah's gentle perfume and began to hear a glockenspiel plunking out the notes of Brahms' Lullaby.

"Have a seat here Ms. Kessler, said Br. Manuel, "I'll let Brother Bede know that you are here."

"You must be Brother Manuel," said Sarah, "I have to tell you that those new Bakewell tarts are awesome!"

"Thank you," said Br. Manuel.

As she waited in the lobby of the abbey, she

began to hear the low thrum of a thunderclap developing somewhere off in the distance. Soon, there were more, and more, and then large, heavy beads of rain. The first droplets began to pelt the walkway outside and then the stained-glass windows of the vestibule. A few strong gusts of wind drove the hard, watery pellets sideways into the window. She felt a bit uneasy, but decided that a stone-walled fortress was a pretty good sanctuary in which to weather a storm.

Br. Philip had been walking in the direction of the lobby and, upon hearing the thunder, decided to take a peek at Mother Nature's fireworks. He was startled by the presence of Sarah in the lobby, but managed to offer an awkward introduction and explanation for his presence.

"Hello," he said, "I am Brother Philip. I heard the commotion and had to see what's going on. Whoa, this looks like a doozy. Are you here to see the Abbot?"

"No," she said, I'm here to see Brother Bede, I am Sarah, a therapist from the clinic and I was hoping to have a word with him. He is supervising my work."

There was a sudden flash of lightning and a loud boom just as Br. Bede entered the room. The lights flickered, but stayed on. Br. Bede feigned an exaggerated flinch and said "I trust that you have both introduced yourselves. Good, Sarah, we can meet in the library. Brother Philip, I think that Father Albert is looking for you."

In the library, Sarah explained to Br. Bede what had happened. Br. Bede thought over the possibilities.

"Well," he started, "we know that he has anger issues, but he might have some trust issues as well. Hunter wants to be in charge of the relationship. And then he doesn't. He doesn't trust you yet, and why should he at this point? By coming to the appointment early, he put himself in control, and when you wouldn't see him early, that put you back in control."

"The games people play," said Sarah.

"Yes," said Br. Bede, "but I think that he will be back soon."

At that point the lights flickered again and this time went out. It was late afternoon, but the sky was so dark that it looked like nighttime in the old room. "Oh," said Sarah, "this can't be good."

"Sure it can, said Br. Bede. We are grateful for everything the Lord gives us, even storms. This will water our plants and help to wash the dirt away. Also, we now have an opportunity to receive light, and a gentle scent from the candles made by Br. Canisius. In his spare time, he likes to make candles for the abbey. We use them a lot, you know."

The abbey did not have a back-up generator, but always had enough candles available to ensure that darkness could not last long. Br. Canisius himself soon appeared with a boxful of candles and a modern click lighter. He lit a few candles. Sarah appeared a bit surprised by the plastic lighter. Br. Canisius noticed her surprise. "We are not Amish," Ms. Kessler," he said, "we have nothing against modern conveniences, as long as they don't take our minds off of the Lord."

Now the room glowed with a soft golden light. From the outside, thought Sarah, this must look like a Thomas Kinkaid painting. Br. Bede resumed the discussion about Hunter Stephenson. "Sarah," he said, "it would seem that you have two choices. You could contact him and ask him why he left, or you could wait to see if he contacts you. Which do you think would be the wiser course of action?"

"It's so tempting for me to contact him first, but I don't think that that would be wise."

"Why not," asked Br. Bede."

"Because if he is ever to grow up, he will need to begin taking more responsibility for his behavior," she said, "that is exactly what got him into this mess."

"Bingo," said Br. Bede. "I don't think you'll have to wait long. Remember, he's on probation."

As Br. Bede walked Ms. Kessler to the door, he noticed someone lurking in a nearby recess in the hallway. It was Br. Philip.

CHAPTER 12

The thunderstorm had passed and the air was ripe with the thick smells of heaven and earth. Drops of rain descended slowly from the trees like melting pearls, a gentle coda in counterpoint to the fury of the main event. Br. Philip had been summoned once again to the abbot's chamber for a discussion of his progress or lack thereof. To his own surprise, Br. Philip found himself looking forward to his meeting. Fr. Albert greeted him warmly and offered him a cup of tea. "Do you mind Earl Grey?" he asked.

Br. Philip accepted the tea and before the abbot could say a word, he blurted: "Mixed progress."

"Tell me more brother," said the abbot, sounding more like a therapist than a priest, "let's hear some details."

Br. Philip said that his prayers seem to be giving

him strength to control his verbal outbursts a little better. He was very tempted at breakfast this morning to make a comment when Fr. Berthold had loudly passed gas, but, with great effort, he was able to stifle his impulse. Also, during Compline, when Br. Manuel was reading the scriptures, Br. Philip had another impulse on which he did not act. "When Brother Manuel read the words 'Let he who is without sin cast the first stone,' I wanted so bad to fling a pebble at his head – but I didn't."

"Okay," said Fr. Albert, "I guess that's progress...of a sort. I encourage you to continue to pray on it, as well as to practice more self-control. Now, you said that your progress has been mixed. How so?"

"It's the lust thing, father. I try to push such thoughts out of my mind, but they pop back in at the most inopportune times. For example, I just met the new therapist, Sarah, and I was instantly smitten with her. Br. Bede told me that you wanted to see me, but I hung out near the library in order to get another peek at the woman. I know that it's sinful, but what can I do?"

"Smitten, was it?" smiled the abbot. "I can think of other words to better describe your condition at that moment. You know, it is said that St. Benedict himself struggled with that very same demon, but apparently his lust was much stronger than yours. In fact, whenever his sexual feelings began to overwhelm him, he would strip naked and roll his body around in a nettle patch. Do you know what a nettle patch is?" asked the abbot. Without waiting for an answer, the abbot said, "The nettle is a nasty little plant that stings and burns when it comes in contact with human skin. St. Benedict rolled around in it until the pain drove out his lust, reportedly forever."

"Should I find a nettle patch?" asked Br. Philip.

"No Philip, I don't even know if the story is true, it might be apocryphal. But either way, it is a good metaphor for the pain one must endure in order to become more Christlike. When you chose to enter the order, you knew it would not be easy, well, here you are. Even living in a monastery, our modern life will sometimes put you in the presence of an attractive woman. You will need to develop a different way of responding to such temptations."

Br. Philip considered that perhaps the nettle patch would be a quicker and less painful remedy.

"Thank you, Father," said Br. Philip. He paused while deciding whether he should ask the question that was waiting on his tongue like a horse at the gate. He decided to go for it.

"Abbot, the last time we talked, there were some things heavy on your mind. You know, the collapse of western civilization, the "untethered" generation and things like that. Can we talk some more about that? I hate to see you so sad and, who knows, maybe a younger perspective might help."

Fr. Albert had hoped that his young brother would want to talk again. After their last chat, he had experienced a catharsis of sorts, not just from his tears, but perhaps more from the brief bonding with a brother who was humbled by his own doubts. Fr. Albert's view of the world had not changed, but he felt that his sense of discouragement had somehow been lessened. Is this acceptance, he wondered? Or surrender?

"Father, I was thinking since the last time we talked. Maybe you are disappointed because you have lived so many years in such a different world. I have not. This is sort of what the world has looked like all of my life. I know many of the people out there. They are not bad people; they just had the misfortune of growing up at a time when Christian values are treated like shit. Excuse my French. It's like this, nature abhors a vacuum and without Christ, people seek other values to fill the void.

"Their values come from their lack of grace, lack of Christ. We are lucky. Christians believe in forgiveness, humility, mercy and gratefulness. These things give us a very profound sense of peace. Without Christ as the anchor, modern people have replaced forgiveness with the hollow call for "justice" which really means revenge. They replace humility with a need for power and attention. They show mercy to no one. They replace gratefulness with envy and greed, a desire for all that they do not possess, such as power, material things. There is also a lack of accountability for their own choices and lifestyles. No one has the guts to call it what it is: immature, selfish, tantrum-like behavior based on emotion and not thought."

"Great Caesar's ghost!" said Fr. Albert. "Who are you and what have you done with Brother Philip?

"Hey," said Br. Philip, I might be a sinner, but I'm not stupid."

"No, you are not, my brother," said Fr. Albert.

"In fact, I am quite impressed with your ability to see things so clearly, and to understand the spiritual shortcomings of modern culture. Perhaps you can use that talent to address your own difficulties in following Christ. Can you see how that might help? Right now, your emotions in certain areas are stronger than your intellect. But with that exceptional brain of yours, it shouldn't take long for the situation to be reversed. Use the talents that God has given you and you will soon become stronger in your faith."

"Thank you, Abbot Albert, I will try," said Br. Philip.

As he left the abbot's chamber, Br. Philip felt a renewed sense of confidence in his abilities. It's one thing to think that you are smart, but it is another to hear it said by a person you admire. Br. Philip felt as light as a feather, and as the church bells rang seven times, he gently struck his breast in unison to each note. I think I'm starting to get it, he thought to himself. Yes, he was.

CHAPTER 13

Sarah Kessler arrived at the clinic not knowing what to expect. It had been one week since Hunter Stephenson had skipped out on his appointment. She had not called him, taking the clinically sound position that he needed to begin taking responsibility for himself, and any outreach on her part would absolve him of that duty. Mrs. McNulty greeted her with the usual "And how might this lovely day find you, Ms. Kessler?"

Sarah acknowledged the greeting and Mrs. McNulty informed her that she had a message. "Ms. Holliday of the probation department requests that you call her regarding that little brat Hunter Stephenson."

"Now, now, Mrs. McNulty," said Sarah, "we shouldn't talk about our clients in such terms. We need to show them respect." She purposely used the pronoun "we" so as to soften the rebuke.

"I show respect to those who earn it, Ms. Kessler, and just so you know, you have not been here nearly long enough to chastise my behavior."

"OK, Mrs. McNulty," said Sarah, "I have been forewarned."

Sarah returned the call to Ms. Holliday who filled her in on the absence of Hunter Stephenson. It seems that after he left the St. Adelaide Guidance Center last week, he had joined a small group of like-minded friends who had conspired to spray-paint the *Spirit of Detroit* statue with some obscene opinions regarding capitalism. They spelled the word capitalism with a *u* after the *t,* which gave their commentary a completely novel meaning. The perpetrators did the deed in broad daylight and were immediately arrested by Detroit's finest, with live television coverage provided by *TV2 Fox News Detroit.* This time, being his second offense, he did not get off with the easy option of therapy only. Instead, the judge gave him a five-hundred dollar fine, two-hundred hours of community service and a stipulation that he return to therapy immediately. Ms. Holliday informed Sarah that Hunter has asked that his community service be performed in the kitchens of the St. Adelaide Abbey.

"God help us," said Sarah Kessler.

"He always does," said Mrs. McNulty who had been eavesdropping from another room.

CHAPTER 14

A week later, Hunter Stephenson showed up for his appointment with Sarah, this time only ten minutes early. His first words after being brought into Sarah's office were, "I'm sorry for ditching you last week."

Sarah milked a prolonged silence before she said, solemnly, "In nomine patris et filii et spiritus sanctus, I forgive you."

Hunter looked astonished. "Hey, I thought you were Jewish," he said.

"I am," Sarah replied, "but, you know, when in Rome..."

Hunter showed no reaction to this phrase, so she added "...do as the Romans?"

"OK, I get it," he said, but Sarah wasn't so sure.

In psychotherapy, everything that happens is so called *grist for the mill*. Not wanting to let this grist go to waste, she asked Hunter to described everything that had happened between the time she had greeted him an hour early and the time he was arrested. She was hoping that she (and more importantly, he) would find a connection between how he had felt that day in the waiting room and his later acting out in anger.

"OK," he began, "so I waited for you and then I got bored. I mean, I was here for like two hours in the waiting room, and you didn't come out yet, so I left."

Sarah wanted to tell him it was his own fault for coming too early (and, it was only one hour, not two), but she bit her tongue. "OK, go on," she said.

"I went home to, uh, oh, I don't care, I'll just say it, to smoke a joint. There, I said it. Then my roommate Carl came home and we smoked some more. By that time, we were feeling pretty buzzed and then Darryl comes over with some spray paint and asks us if we feel like having some fun. We did, so we hopped in Darryl's Subaru and headed downtown. We looked for something cool to tag and then we saw it. That spirit of *something* statue in front of the City-County building. We walked around it like a couple times, and then when we didn't see anyone looking, we tagged it. Carl dotted the eyes with red paint; Darryl drew a swastika on it and I came in for the coupe da grass – a message I won't repeat here regarding capitalism. Big deal. It was all in fun, we didn't like, hurt anyone."

Sarah looked at Hunter with a sympathetic face that masked her incredulity. "Hunter," she asked, "do you really believe that defacing a public statue was a harmless act, that no one was hurt by your behavior? Here is what I would like you to do. Think for a moment about who might have been affected by what you did and then tell me about it."

Hunter sighed and did as he was told. He thought about it for a while and then said, "OK, like maybe the dudes who had to clean it up, they'd probably be a little bit pissed off."

"Anyone else"?

He thought a little more and said, "I don't know, maybe the guy who owns the statue."

"Good," said Sarah. "That would be you, and me and the other citizens of Detroit. Anyone else?"

"Not really," he said.

"Alright," said Sarah, "at least now we are getting somewhere. So, you do acknowledge that your behavior has had a negative effect on some others. I'm not saying this to accuse you, I am saying it so that maybe in the future, you might think about the effects before you act, not after."

"You sound like my mother."

"Well I'm your therapist, not your mother, but as long as we are on the subject, why don't you tell me about your mother? What is she like?"

Hunter spent the rest of the session telling Sarah about his mother. And his father. Sarah, for the first time began to feel sorry for him. She reminded herself to keep her clinical distance.

"Mom would basically do whatever Dad wanted and then she would drink herself to sleep on the sofa and go to bed. I wouldn't really say we were close."

Hunter described his father as a cold man with a

temper. "Like I said before, he was an asshole. I didn't like him much and I don't think he really liked me either. He never hit me or anything, but sometimes I wished that he would have, so that I could punch him in the face. The day I left home was the day he told me to get a job and start paying rent to live in my own bedroom."

Sarah was beginning to see the motivation behind the man.

CHAPTER 15

After his therapy session was over, Hunter walked across the parking lot and entered St. Adelaide Abbey to begin his community service. He was met by Br. Manuel who, upon greeting the young man, immediately heard the distinct and unpleasant sound of the grinding of teeth, a sound he always heard when in the presence of marijuana or patchouli. It was embedded in Hunter's clothing. Hiding his revulsion, Br. Manuel showed Hunter around the kitchen and introduced him to Br. Philip who would supervise his work. Fr. Albert had decided that Br. Philip's spiritual growth would benefit from having responsibility for someone other than himself. Also, Br. Philip was much closer in age to Hunter than any of the other monks.

Br. Philip said hello to his new charge and

Hunter responded with "Hey, I didn't know there were young monks! I thought that they were all old and bald. You look young and you have a full head of hair."

"Yes," said Br. Philip, "I am younger than most, but that bald head you refer to is called a tonsure, and we are not required to do that anymore. Unless we want to. So, Hunter, I understand that you are here to serve out your community service requirement. What did you do to deserve such a draconian sentence?"

"Does draconian mean like Dracula," he asked?

"Something like that," answered Br. Philip.

Well," he said, "I was already on probation for accidentally knocking an old lady over at a demonstration, and then I got caught tagging that spirit statue downtown with an obscenity. The judge could have thrown me in jail but instead, she threw me here. No offense, man."

"No offense taken," said Br. Philip. "Work is work no matter where you do it, and work is good for the soul. Not to pry, but do you have any kind of religious preference?"

"Yeah, I'd prefer not to," he joked.

Br. Philip didn't laugh. He knew that most young people these days did not have a solid religious grounding. Despite Br. Philip's own current struggles, he knew without question, that his faith gave him strength and purpose. He also knew that without the grace of God, Hunter was doomed. "Let's make some tarts," he said.

First, they rolled the dough by hand, using the old hardwood rolling pins that were seasoned veterans of all the prior tarting campaigns. These pins had seen it all, from the first simple marmalade tarts to the questionable experiments with mangos and kiwis, to the latest iteration of the delicious, best-selling Bakewell tarts. Br. Philip showed Hunter how to hand-roll the raw, virgin dough into perfect slabs of pastry, not too heavy, not too thin, but just the right thickness to balance the scrumptiousness within. Hunter caught on quickly and was soon able to create reasonably workable slabs of dough.

After that, Br. Philip showed Hunter how to fill the slabs with just the right amount of filler: marmalade or whatever, to roll them up, and then to crimp the edges into self-contained pockets of ambrosial bliss. Hunter seemed to enjoy the process of working with his hands, turning raw materials into something that might eventually be of value to everyday people. He had never before experienced a connection between his efforts and a positive outcome.

After Br. Philip showed Hunter how to bake the tarts to perfection, the result was glorious. The tarts smelled and tasted like nothing Hunter had ever before experienced. He was astounded. He had produced something wonderful. Why, he wondered, had no one taught him this before?

Working next to them today were Brs. Bede and Canisius. Fr. Berthold sat in a corner chair taking in all of the activity. His "baker emeritus" status allowed him to abstain from work while remaining close to his brothers.

"I go cuckoo for Cocoa Puffs," stated the old

monsignor.

"What's with the old fossil," asked Hunter?

Br. Bede responded before Br. Philip or Br. Canisius could open their mouths.

"That, son, is Father Berthold, the oldest and most respected member of our community. The man that you condescendingly refer to as a fossil is a man who has devoted his life to God and this brotherhood. He has taught us more than you will ever know, and if you ever call him a fossil again, I'll knock you on your ass."

"Brother Bede," said Br. Philip, "take it easy on him, he is just a kid. He doesn't know any better."

"I bet he does now," replied Br. Bede.

Br. Bede was right, at that moment the young Hunter Stevenson had learned at least one valuable lesson: don't make fun of someone who has a twelve-foot tall friend standing next to him.

Br. Bede left the kitchen and Br. Philip turned to the frightened young man. "Hunter," he said, "Brother Bede is right, you know. It's not cool to make fun of old people, or really anyone, for that matter. God loves us all and that includes you, me, Br. Bede and Fr. Berthold. Have you noticed that the brothers living in this monastery seem to be content, if not happy, most of the time? There is a reason for that. We have a purpose in life. We serve the Lord and do his work. In return, he blesses us with things you could never buy."

"Like what?"

"Good question," said Br. Philip. "Things like gratefulness, forgiveness and humility. You wouldn't believe the misery caused by the opposite.

People who hold grudges and don't forgive others carry around the heaviest baggage on earth. They stay angry and spiteful sometimes for their entire lives. People who are not grateful for the blessings they have, also spend their lives angry, depressed and resentful of others. That's some heavy baggage too. Humility is a little harder to understand but, trust me, it provides a lot more peace to the soul than pride ever did."

Br. Bede returned to the kitchen and approached Hunter. Hunter winced a little, not knowing what to expect, but Br. Bede thrust his hand out and said, "I'm sorry Mr. Stevenson, it was not right for me to talk to you in that manner. Will you please forgive my outburst? Again, I am sorry."

Hunter, having already been chastised by Br. Philip, replied, "I'm sorry too, for calling Father Berthold a...a...a, well he seems like a good guy anyway. I'll accept your apology if you accept mine."

"Done," said Br. Bede as the church bells rang out for the start of vespers.

CHAPTER 16

Fr. Albert decided that he needed some fresh air and a little exercise. He laced up his comfortable walking shoes, grabbed his favorite meerschaum pipe, and headed casually up the street toward Woodward Avenue. Nowadays, outdoors was the only place that he could smoke his pipe anymore, as even religious orders had banned the demon tobacco from inside their walls. Damned Nazis, he thought. Fascists. He puffed contentedly as he ambled along, taking in whiffs of the redolent vanilla Cavendish smoke between carefully measured steps. Wispy puffs of fragrant ghosts comforted his beleaguered soul. Six months ago, he had misjudged a curb and suffered a terrible sprain in his foot, leading to his current hyper-attentiveness while walking.

Fr. Albert could see in the distance that some

sort of frenzied communal activity was occurring on Woodward. A parade, he thought, but it was now mid-June and there were no holidays this time of year as far as he could remember. As he got closer, he could see no floats or bands, but there were signs, banners and much colorful clothing. And lots of yelling. When he finally reached Woodward, it was clear that he now found himself smack dab in the middle of a Gay Pride march. There were representatives of all manner of alternate sexual identities strutting proudly down the avenue. A colorful lot it was. Some of the marchers surely considered it an odd sight to see the aged monk in full habit standing in awe by the corner, while an assemblage of gay men, lesbians, various forms of transgender persons and their supporters walked and danced by. One of the female (at least Fr. Albert guessed her to be) members broke rank and came over to greet the father.

"Thank you for coming out to support our cause, Father," she said, while handing him an invitation to an after-parade party.

"Well, I, I don't really..." he began to stutter, "I d-don't really..." he decided it best not to finish his sentence. As a faithful Catholic, he certainly could not condone such lifestyles, but then, he thought, God created each of these people and loved them as he loved all of us. He tried to smile as the technicolor parade shimmied by, but inside, he was once again possessed by his old friend the black dog of depression. This parade and celebration, to Fr. Albert, was just one more sign that the world he knew and treasured, was disintegrating. Sodom and

Gomorrah redux. He turned and walked back toward the abbey, a place that now seemed more of a sanctuary than ever before. After walking just a few feet, a plastic water bottle whizzed past, inches from his head, and he heard someone say, "You'll burn in hell with all of the other haters, holy man!"

Another man from the march sprinted past Fr. Albert and picked up the bottle. "I'm sorry brother, not all of us are jerks."

CHAPTER 17

The next morning Fr. Albert went missing. At some point between lauds and prime, Br. Manuel noticed that the abbot had not been seen since matins. "Have you seen Father Albert?" he asked Br. Bede.

"No," said Br. Bede, "he was there for matins, I'm sure, but beyond that, I don't think I've seen him. That's odd. It's not like him."

The monks did a search inside the myriad nooks and crannies of the abbey hoping to find the Abbot sleeping or holed up somewhere reading his Bible. As the search went on, anxiety began to replace hope as each man feared that they would find him injured or worse, God forbid. They searched the grounds and the Guidance Center to no avail. Inside the abbot's room they found that his pipe and tobacco were gone, as were his wallet, walking shoes and his well-worn leather Bible.

"Wherever he went," observed Br. Canisius, "it looks like he went voluntarily. He took all of his favorite things. Maybe he just forgot to tell anyone that he had to go somewhere."

Just then, Br. Philip came in and asked, "Did anyone take the Tartmobile? I was just going to do a bread run, but the Aztek is gone."

No one answered but they each looked at one another knowingly. It became clear to all that the abbot had absconded with the Tartmobile.

"Well, at least," said Br. Philip "he should be easy enough to find."

Br. Bede called some of the places he thought Fr. Albert might have gone; The Avalon Bakery, his nephew's house, the Archbishop. None of those panned out and the brothers were soon out of ideas. Br. Philip suggested making a missing person report, but they all agreed that you can't call the police to say that a grown man who is not senile, and clearly left voluntarily, is missing.

Fr. Berthold ambled down the hallway and stopped when he came upon the group of worried monks. He perused their furled brows and calmly smiled. "He'll be back," he said, as clear as a church-bell.

CHAPTER 18

It was still dark when Fr. Albert turned the key of the venerable old Pontiac. He hoped that no one would hear the grinding of the engine turning over or the crisp sound of the gravel crunching under the wheels. He stealthily kept the lights off until he was out of the abbey compound. When he finally turned the lights on, he was startled to see the illuminated form of a young prostitute attempting to sell her body as if it were the fresh catch of the day.

The young siren waved and smiled at him but he drove on, trying his best not to look her in the eye. I am no better than she, he thought, sneaking out under the cover of darkness to run away. But why am I running, he wondered? He drove for a few minutes in silence. His mind was heavy, as if pregnant with a thought to which he could not give birth.

The Abbot turned the wheel of the bright yellow Aztek and set a course for I-75. He knew where he was going but not entirely why. His driving skills were a bit rusty and he was pre-occupied. At the next stoplight he lightly bumped into the rear end of a stationary Chrysler 300 in front of him. As he got out of the car to check for damage, the occupant of the other car had also exited his vehicle and was walking toward him. Quickly. With raised voice, and a clenched fist, the enraged man approached him and asked the gentle priest "What the hell were you thinking, you idiot? "

A few more ripe adjectives were hurled in the abbot's general direction until the driver noticed that Fr. Albert was a man of the cloth. "Figures," he said, "a damned priest." The man inspected his plastic bumper and determined that there was, in fact, no damage at all.

Fr. Albert apologized profusely to the man. "I'm sorry, I'm so sorry," he said. "I had my mind on other things and I didn't notice the light."

"You're a moron," continued the belligerent man, "a menace on the road. Stay far, far away from me." With that, the man got back into his car, slammed the door and squealed his tires for maximum effect. The sound evoked in Fr. Albert's mind the very demons of hell. Meanwhile, the drivers behind the abbot began to impatiently honk their horns, making the street sound much like it did the last time the hapless Tigers won the World Series in 1984.

Fr. Albert got back into his car and wondered if

the man was right. "Maybe I am an idiot, or a moron, whichever is worse." He tried to remember the early terms used by psychologists in the nineteenth century to describe those who suffered cognitive disabilities. I remember, he said to himself, idiots were the worst, followed by imbeciles and then morons. Well, he thought, I hope that I am least a moron.

On the ramp to I-75 North, Fr. Albert was careful to merge safely onto the freeway before letting out a breath and settling in for the long drive up north. The last twenty-four hours had confirmed his not entirely unwarranted belief that most of the world's problems can be traced to its big cities. Too many people, too little space, too many problems, no room for God. Cities, he thought, were frenzied at all times, leaving no space for quiet solitude. He remembered another quote from Thomas Merton: "It is good to be quiet enough to let God work." And so he did.

The abbot drove in silence for the next hour. He occasionally prayed quietly that the Lord would show him why he had taken this unexpected pilgrimage. He thought of all the recent events in his life. The talks with Br. Philip, the endless protests in the streets, the Gay Pride parade, the prostitute on Woodward, the man who had come close to assaulting him for a minor fender-bender minus the bent fender. Black Dog was back and Fr. Albert was beginning to question why God was allowing his world to fall to pieces. He let himself wallow in despair for a while, but it didn't last long. He was abruptly brought out of his funk when a car passed him with a bumper sticker that read: HONK IF YOU LOVE JESUS – TEXT AND DRIVE IF YOU WANT TO MEET HIM. Fr. Albert began to laugh. He marveled at how such a small thing could so quickly pull him out of himself and give him some perspective. "Thanks, Lord, I needed that!" he said out loud.

CHAPTER 19

Hunter's second day of community service went better than the first. Today, the monks were making apricot tarts topped with a generous sprinkling of powdered sugar. The familiar smell put Hunter into a comforting reverie, where he regressed to the innocent child being served treats by his doting grandmother.

Grandma Stephenson always made apricot tarts when he stayed with her for weekends or for weeks in the summer. She was so kind and attentive that Hunter wondered how that sweet woman could have produced his father.

Br. Manuel announced his arrival upon entering the kitchen. "Choo, Choo, Choo, I can hear the Apricot Express coming down the tracks."

Br. Manuel didn't know why he associated certain smells with specific sounds. Since he had been that way for most of his life, he just accepted it. He didn't question it any more than a "normal" person would question their memory of pine needles and Christmas. His apricot association was that of his childhood Lionel train, clacking around the metal track in his basement. It seems that apricots and model trains can sometimes take different men to the same place.

The tone among the brotherhood was subdued. All were worried about Abbot Albert, who had been gone for hours without calling or otherwise contacting them. Br. Philip was perhaps the most affected by Fr. Albert's absence. The two men had bonded somewhat over their recent counseling sessions, although it remained unclear exactly who was counseling whom. Br. Philip felt that he was indeed beginning to mature, slightly, as he drew closer to the Lord. He wasn't so sure that his efforts to cheer up the abbot were as successful. The last time he saw Fr. Albert, the man looked as morose as a fellow just given his last meal on death row – and it was fried Spam.

Br. Canisius arrived jangling a set of car keys. He had been able to borrow another van from the Avalon Bakery and was ready to load it up. Br. Philip was now off of restrictions and was ready to accompany his friend on the bread run. At the last moment he had a change of heart. "Canisius, why don't you take Hunter with you this time? You could show him the other side of our work."

Br. Canisius agreed and so the monk and the not-so-juvenile delinquent together loaded the van and drove to the Avalon. Along the way, Hunter asked,

"How come all you guys are so nice all the time?"

Br. Canisius replied in a manner that made it seem that he and Br. Philip had gotten the same memo. "It is our nature to be kind, because our nature comes from the kindest of all, God. Jesus teaches us to be humble, to be thankful for all we have and to forgive others. Once you get the hang of that, the rest is a piece of cake. It's kind of like the secret to happiness. I don't why so many others refuse to accept this secret."

"Yeah," said Hunter, "I guess it's like Pete Townshend said in *Tommy*: 'You've been shown the way before; Messiahs pointed to the door; But no one had the guts to leave the temple.'"

"What," said Br. Canisius, "you're a Who freak? You're too young to even know who they are."

"Hell yes," said Hunter. "Sorry, I mean heck yes. My dad had all of their albums on vinyl. He was gone so much that I had plenty of time to listen to them full blast."

"What would you think," asked Br. Canisius, "if I told you that I was a roadie on The Who's last U.S. tour before I became a monk?"

CHAPTER 20

F r. Albert continued to drive north on I-75 until he cleared Oakland County, the last suburban area of metro Detroit. Traffic had thinned ever so slightly for the next twenty miles or so and then picked up again abruptly as he approached the Flint/Saginaw area. He watched, as cars whizzed past him or tailgated him menacingly whenever he did not acquiesce to the speed demands of the agitated drivers.

Okay, we're back in the city now, he thought, help me, St. Christopher, wherever you are. He wondered what it was about city driving that changed mild-mannered accountants and schoolteachers into murderous maniacs in a hellish death race. He thought of pulling off the road for a while, but the frightening specter of merging back onto the freeway on another city ramp kept him glued to the wheel. Besides, he thought that he could make it all the way to Indian River without stopping for anything.

There were two things he wanted, no, needed, in Indian River: the cabin and the cross. The former was a small log cabin in a secluded area of Burt Lake. His old friend Jimmy Beauregard, who had attended Sacred Heart Seminary with him, owned the cabin and let Fr. Albert use it whenever he needed some solitude to clear his head. The latter was a twenty-eight-foot-tall wood and bronze crucifix known as The Shrine of the Cross in the Woods. It was said to be the largest crucifix in the world (Christ the Redeemer in Rio de Janeiro was technically a statue of Christ, not a crucifix). Built in 1959, Catholics from around the world visit the shrine, and Fr. Albert has always found comfort under the giant arms of Christ.

When Fr. Albert reached Saginaw, traffic on the freeway came to an unexpected halt. It wasn't a slowdown; it was a complete stoppage. Was it an accident? No. It seems that a group protesting racial injustice had decided to make their point by standing with arms locked across the entire northbound lanes of I-75. While local media would later describe it as a "peaceful protest" the terrified drivers thought otherwise. "Oh, God, what now?" said the exasperated priest. When he saw what was happening, he just sighed.

"Please Lord," he prayed "why don't you just kill us all now and put us out of our misery?" Fr. Albert again bemoaned the breakdown of our culture and at the same time wondered how a group of normal, possibly intelligent people could somehow believe that the way to get others to sympathize with their cause was to bully the innocents and deprive them of their rights. He just didn't get it.

Soon the Michigan State Police troopers arrived to disperse the crowd and restore order. When Fr. Albert finally got a chance to move forward, he floored the accelerator and squealed his tires, just like the man who had accosted him in Detroit. He was surprised that the Tartmobile was capable of such rudeness. "Sorry, Lord," he said, "please forgive me."

CHAPTER 21

Br. Philip was bored again. He needed something to perk him up. He considered pulling another prank on Br. Canisius, but this time he needed a different form of excitement. He decided that he would pay a visit to Sarah Kessler. Today was her day at the Guidance Center and, well, why not? First, he had to come up with a reason to go there so that she wouldn't be suspicious of his motives. What were his motives, he thought? He quickly pushed that notion out of his mind as being irrelevant.

Br. Philip slipped out of the abbey without attracting any attention. He slinked into the lobby like a man entering a dirty book store, and asked Mrs. McNulty if he might have a word with Ms. Kessler.

"And just what might this be regarding, Brother

Philip?" asked the vigilant receptionist/sergeant-at-arms.

"I just want to welcome her to our guidance center and let her know that she has my full support,"
he said.

"Oh, that would be great," said Mrs. McNulty, "I'm sure that she has been crying herself to sleep each night wondering if she has the full support of Brother Philip. I'll see if she is available"

Br. Philip was used to Mrs. McNulty's poison darts, yet he felt a bit more sensitive this time because he knew that he was there under questionable pretenses. He wondered how he would start the conversation and where it might go from there.

"Ms. Kessler will see you now, Brother Philip," said Mrs. McNulty. Under her breath she muttered "Just remember that you are a holy man."

"Brother Philip, this is a surprise," said Sarah, "please come in and have a seat."

"Thank you," said Br. Philip as he sat down, "I just thought I'd stop by and see if you are settling in OK here. Everyone says that you are doing a great job."

Sarah smiled and looked at the young monk. Br. Philip was quite handsome, she thought. He was tall and neither portly (as she imagined all monks to be) nor gaunt. Being young, he had a loose shock of curly blondish hair and an intriguing pair of shimmering green eyes. His impish smile revealed a perfect set of straight and nearly white teeth. If only he wasn't a monk sworn to celibacy, she thought.

"Thank you," she said, "I really like it here and everyone has been really, really kind. What do you do at the monastery?" she asked.

I mainly disappoint people, he thought to himself, but it came out as, "I make the tarts, do the bread runs to the Avalon, and spend the rest of my time in prayer and services – kind of like everyone else here."

Sarah noticed that Br. Philip had a hard time keeping his eyes elevated above her chest. She didn't dress like a nun, but she found it liberating to wear tops that, while chaste by today's standards, might show just enough cleavage to affirm that she was indeed a woman. Now, with Br. Philip's eyes locked on to her breasts, she wondered if, maybe she should tone it down a bit.

"How long have you been at St. Adelaide Abbey?" she asked, now feeling her inner Torquemada rising again.

"About six years now, but I'm still growing into the job," he admitted.

"Aren't we all," she replied. For the next few moments, an awkward silence filled the room with neither party knowing where to go next. Br. Philip decided that he would take the initiative.

"Well Sarah, it was nice to have this little talk, but I have work to do. You know, idle hands are the devil's workshop."

"Yeah," she winked, "you wouldn't want to leave the door open to a dybbuk."

"A what?"

"A dybbuk, in Jewish tradition, is an evil spirit that enters a person's body, and you can guess the hilarity that follows."

Br. Philip laughed and thought to himself, that's it, I'm a goner now, she's funny, too. He said a polite goodbye and headed out to the lobby where, under the watchful eyes of Mrs. McNulty, he made his exit. He was certain that he had made another stupid mistake.

CHAPTER 22

Br. Canisius didn't know why he had lied to Hunter. He had never been a roadie for The Who, so what made him say that? Did he fib because he wanted to pull Hunter's leg a bit, or was there some darker motive? Oh, what a tangled web he had weaved, because now Hunter was pumping him for stories about Roger Daltrey and Pete Townshend. Having the opportunity to fess-up and tell Hunter the truth, Br. Canisius, instead, chose to change the subject as they pulled into a parking spot near the bakery.

"Hello Brother Canisius," said Carla, "who's this, a new monk in training?"

"No, Carla, this is Hunter, he'll be helping us out in the abbey kitchen for a while." He saw no need to embarrass the young man by revealing his community service obligation.

"Well, welcome," said Carla, "you can start right now by helping Brother Canisius load this bread into the van.

"Hey," she yelled, "where is the yellow Tartmobile? Did it get stolen?"

"Naw," he lied, "Fr. Albert just borrowed it for a little while, so your boss let me borrow one of your bread trucks until he gets back."

Br. Canisius had just lied three times to two people within the last fifteen minutes. He didn't understand what was happening to him. Were they all "little white lies" he wondered, harmless stories to grease the social interactions? What about the bogus roadie tale? That certainly seemed unnecessary. He decided that he would come clean to Hunter later. In the grand scheme of things. what harm had it done?

CHAPTER 23

Fr. Albert arrived at the cabin before noon. Despite the traffic problems, he had made good time. There was plenty of daylight left. He dropped his few belongings onto the old wooden Adirondack chair in the living room and made himself a cup of Earl Grey tea. He would relax and say a rosary before heading over to the cross. His rosary was a beautiful thing to behold.

The beads were simple octagons, but large and deeply lacquered, made of well-figured olive wood from the Holy Land. The intricate silver centerpiece bore the likeness of St. Benedict, and the crucifix was hand carved by an artisan from Medjugorje. It had been given to Fr. Albert by his mother upon his ordination.

When he finished the rosary, Fr. Albert stuffed a plug of fresh vanilla/bourbon tobacco into his meerschaum pipe, fired it up and sank into the big threadbare easy-chair to reflect for a while. That's why he was there, wasn't it? To think. Fr. Albert liked solitude; it was one of the reasons he became a monk. Certainly not the primary reason, but nonetheless important. Then again, he mused, even monks don't get enough time away from others. Between the shared liturgy of the hours, all of the masses and the work that must be done, monks are together far more than they are apart.

Feeling gloriously bored for the first time in ages, Fr. Albert rooted through the magazine basket next to the easy chair. There, he found five ancient *Mad* magazines, three *Field and Streams*, a few old *Time* magazines and a small supply of very outdated *Playboys* and *Hustlers* that he did not care to count. Jimmy Beauregard had dropped out of the seminary long before graduation to the priesthood. Fr. Albert was not interested in the girlie magazines, but this gave him the nudge he needed to leave the cozy chair and head out to the Cross in the Woods.

The shrine was just a short drive from the cabin and not too busy this time of the day. Fr. Albert made his way to the seating area which consisted of a couple dozen wooden park benches arranged like pews, and facing the cross. Fr. Albert surveyed the crowd and chose the bench with the least number of people nearby. He made a sign-of-the-cross and began to pray. As he did, an old woman sat down not three feet from him, even though there were many empty benches all over the park. Fr. Albert thought that the woman looked Polish or Italian judging from the nylon stockings that she had rolled down to the top of her heavy black shoes. He gave her a certain look, which she immediately misinterpreted as an invitation, and began to chat him up.

"Beautiful day, isn't it, father?" she noted.

Fr. Albert nodded but did not answer.

"Doesn't the Lord look lovely today with the bright sun shining down on him?" she continued. "I like to watch the faces of all the pilgrims as they bathe in the Lord's glory. Would you like a piece of my Tootsie Roll?"

"No thank you," he said tersely.

"I have other candy if you don't like Tootsie Rolls, she said. I've got Skittles and Gummy Bears, a Nestle's Crunch bar, Butterfingers and, if I dig deep enough, I might find that elusive box of Milk Duds."

"Thanks," he said, "but I prefer to be alone now so that I can pray."

"OK," the woman said, "I don't need to be told twice. I won't bother you again."

"Thank you," he replied with relief.

"But if you need me, father, I'll be just one bench over."

The woman moved a few feet over to the end of the bench adjacent to where Fr. Albert sat. She smiled and gave him a "toodle loo" wave.

"Lord," he prayed, "I came here for peace. Please let me have some."

Fr. Albert closed his eyes so as to shut out any distractions and to finally be alone with the Lord. It didn't last long. The old woman was back, this time offering him a fresh, cool bottle of water.

"You looked thirsty," she said, and sat down again next to him.

Fr. Albert, although irked, was at heart, a kind man. And also, truth be told, a little thirsty. He thought that the woman was probably lonely, as many older people were. He decided to abandon his silent prayer for now, and talk to the woman. He also ventured a guess that she had not intruded into his space randomly, but rather was sent there because God wanted her to be there at that moment. Just that quickly, his mood changed from irritation to gratefulness that God had chosen to use him to help this stranger.

"Thank you for the water," he said. Please, sit down and join me, we'll enjoy this moment together."

The woman sat down and smiled. She introduced herself as Grace, and Fr. Albert immediately knew that he had guessed right - she was Italian. In growing up, it seemed that all of his female relatives were named either Rose or Grace.

"She asked for his name. "I am Father Albert Costello," he said, "I live at the St. Adelaide Abbey in Detroit and I'm here for a little R & R. Do you live around here?"

"Oh, no," she said, "I'm also from your neck of the woods, so to speak. I come up here every now and then to see the cross and to people-watch. If I'm lucky I'll get to talk to a few people."

"How is the people-watching going today?"

"Not so good," she said, "I can see lots of them, but few of them want to talk to a strange old lady like me."

"Well, you seem nice enough to me," he fibbed. "How has life been treating you?" he asked, expecting to open the door to what she really wanted from him. Maybe she needed money, or just needed a shoulder to cry on. Whatever, this would give the poor woman an opening to tell him what she needed.

"Just fine," she replied, "never felt better, not a care in the world."

Fr. Albert was surprised by her answer. He had expected to hear a long litany of sorrows and complaints, maybe even a jeremiad of sorts. He looked at her and discerned that she was not lying. She really did look content, if not happy.

Grace abruptly rose up and held out her hand. "Thank you for your time Father Albert of Sweet Marmalade Abbey, it has been a pleasure, but I must go now."

Fr. Albert shook her hand and watched her disappear into the distance. I guess she really is from Detroit, he thought, I never mentioned the Abby's nickname, but she was clearly familiar with us. Very strange encounter though, he thought. Maybe it was just a weird coincidence and God hadn't sent Grace to him for any special reason. He returned to his silent prayer and thanked God for the opportunity anyway.

CHAPTER 24

Br. Canisius and Hunter returned to the abbey and unloaded the fresh bread. When they had finished, Hunter said, "Hey, you never told me the details about being a roadie. What was it like?"

Br. Canisius was caught. He now had a choice. He could either confess and come clean, or dig his grave deeper by embellishing his first lie. He chose the former. "I'm sorry Hunter, I was just pulling your leg. I never worked as a roadie and I have never met any members of The Who.'

"Then why did you say that you did?"

"I don't really know," said Br. Canisuis.

It seemed like a minor thing to Br. Canisus, but it was not to Hunter. The young man's face grew ugly with anger, and after a few seconds of silence, he said "Great. Now I'm being lied to by monks. You are just like everyone else, you damn hypocrite. You are an asshole, just like everyone else in my life. I quit."

Br. Canisius tried to apologize, but Hunter would have none of it. He ran towards the door to leave, but then stopped and turned back. He grabbed a heavy metal meat tenderizer that was on the cutting board, and hurled it in the general direction of Br. Canisius cranium (Br. Bede was not present to intervene). Br. Canisius was able to duck in time to avoid serious injury to himself, but the missile struck a gas line connected to the stove, with such force that the line broke open and began to spew natural gas into the room. Br. Canisus ran quickly to shut off the gas valve, but didn't make it in time. The explosion hurled him backward with surprising force, smashing his head into a granite table and instantly knocking him unconscious. Hunter was long gone when other monks rushed into the room with fire extinguishers and buckets of water. Br. Manuel called 911. Br. Philip was able to find the shut-off valve, but he couldn't turn it off. It had been painted over and it wouldn't budge. All the while, gas continued to vent into the room. Finally, Br. Bede appeared with a large wrench and, with great effort, was able to shut the gas valve. When the last of the flames were extinguished, the men looked at the damage. Br. Canisius was still unconscious, but breathing lightly. His face was blackened, but the extent of any other injuries was unknown. Damage to the kitchen was extensive and it looked as though there would be no marmalade tarts produced at the abbey for quite some time. Fr.

Berthold surveyed the scene and, quoting the poet Milton, announced: "*Long is the way, and hard, that out of hell, leads up to light.*"

CHAPTER 25

Br. Philip was inconsolable. Fr. Albert was still missing, and Br. Canisius remained in a coma at Detroit Receiving Hospital. It had only been three days since the accident, but Br. Philip was not sure if he would ever see the two men again.

The monks of St. Adelaide Abbey, despite their loss, continued to pray the liturgy of the hours. Now, perhaps more than ever, the unchanging nature of monastic life helped to fill a void and give meaning to the monk's daily routine. In the absence of Fr. Albert, Br. Bede stepped up to ensure a smooth transition of leadership at this sorrowful time. His first act had been to arrange for at least one monk to remain at Br. Canisius' bedside twenty-fours a day, on rotation, in case he might awaken from his sleep.

Br. Bede called a meeting so the brothers could receive an update on the situation. The mood was somber, with even Br. Philip giving his full attention.

"As you know," said Br. Bede, "I have been in close contact over the past few days with the medical team at Receiving. Our beloved brother is stable and breathing, but the doctors cannot predict when, or even if, he will come out of the coma. Thank you all for keeping the vigil at his side, and for all of the many prayers you have offered in his name.

"Next, I am looking into how we might, with God's help, raise the money we need to repair the kitchen and purchase new stoves and equipment. It is no secret that our funds are very low and it will take a miracle to replace what has been lost. Still, we are grateful that no one else was hurt, and that the abbey did not burn down.

"Finally, I'm sorry to say that I have yet to hear from Father Albert, and I don't know where he is, or where he has gone. All we can do is pray. That is all I have for now. Are there any questions?"

The brothers were silent.

"OK," said Br. Bede, "it is the hour of Terce, so let us continue on our faithful journey. Wait, one more thing. Hey, let's be holy out there."

A few men smiled at the nod to Fr. Albert, but none chuckled.

CHAPTER 26

Br. Philip went back to his room and wept. Unlike some of the other monks, Br. Philip came from a warm and loving family. He was feeling very sad now, and thought of the comfort he had often received from his parents, and especially his mother. Once, when he was in his late teens, he had been dumped by a girlfriend whom he adored. He remembered his mother wordlessly holding him in her arms while he sobbed. Her consolation was morphine to his pain. At this moment, he missed her terribly.

As he thought of his mother, Br. Philip's mind again wandered off-course and conjured up the apparition of a different woman, Sarah Kessler. Being an educated man, Br. Philip recognized that his associative leap from mother memory to fantasy-crush might have revealed a Freudian motivation of sorts. He quickly dismissed that idea as voodoo psychobabble. After all, he thought, Freud never did a scientific experiment in his life. All of his theories came strictly from his fertile, if not twisted, imagination.

Br. Philip's rationalization did the trick. The specter of Sigmund Freud had been banished. Free now of Victorian guilt, Philip resolved to once again pay a visit to the lovely Ms. Kessler tomorrow, when she would be at the guidance center. Maybe she wouldn't hold him tight to her bosom, but he could at least look at it.

CHAPTER 27

Fr. Albert was on his way home. As he wheeled the Tartmobile back onto I-75, south this time, he wondered what his misplaced hegira had accomplished. The world was still decadent, he thought. It hadn't, and probably never would, turn away from its sinful ways. He was also unchanged. He took stock of his current feelings and recognized the same despondency as before. Nothing was different. He still despaired of the current state of western culture and held little hope that things would change for the better. The change he had envisioned, had not happened. And probably never would as long as the newer generations remained untethered to family, faith and history. Still, he ate an orange and drove toward Sweet Marmalade Abbey.

There were no social justice blockades this time,

and the ride home proved to be uneventful. He exited the freeway, pulled into the abbey parking lot and strode into the building as if nothing had happened and he had just returned from a morning stroll. His first surprise as he walked into the monastery was the distinct smell of burnt wood and the residue of an electrical fire. What, in the name of God has happened, he wondered.

Most of the men were at vespers, but Br. Manuel heard the door creak open and went to see who it was. Br. Manuel encountered Fr. Albert and hugged the abbot with gusto while welcoming him home. Br. Manuel smelled the orange that Fr. Albert had been eating and immediately heard Jimmy Buffet singing a forgettable generic tropical song. Next was Fr. Berthold who greeted the abbot with "You've come a long way, baby." They both smiled. That was a language everyone understood.

When word spread through the abbey that Fr. Albert was back, all of the monks quickly gathered to welcome him home. He was surprised at the intensity of their emotions and felt himself tearing up as well. Br. Philip seemed the happiest of all.

"I have something important to show you," said Br. Philip "once you get settled in."

Br. Bede joined the celebratory throng and asked to meet with Fr. Albert alone, so as to fill him in on the events of the week.

The two men left the others and entered the abbot's room where each settled into the waiting chairs of comfort. "So," began the abbot, "who burned the damned place down?"

"I'll get to that in a moment," said Br. Bede, "but

first, where have you been father?"

"I took a spontaneous trip," he said. "I had to get away from this crazy world for a while, to clear my head. I went up to a friend's cabin on a lake that will remain anonymous. I prayed, I smoked my pipe and had a few drams of the single malt Scotch I found in the cupboard. Lagavooloo or something, I think."

"Is it *us* driving you to drink? Is it the abbey?

"No, Brother Bede," said Fr. Albert, it's not you or the abbey. In fact, this is the only place that seems sane these days. Walk out of these doors and you take your life in your hands. Or your soul. Maybe both. Anyway, it didn't help. It was nice to have a little more solitude than normal, but I now stand, or sit, before you just as disillusioned with our planet as I was when I left."

Br. Bede felt empathy for the abbot's plight, but didn't understand why Fr. Albert was so concerned about the outside world. Wasn't that the point of monastic life, he thought? To be away from the everyday concerns of the world so as to be focused solely on Christ? Still, it was clear that Fr. Albert was in need of comfort.

"Let me get you a nice cup of Earl Grey tea and a fresh Bakewell tart," said Br. Bede. "Then I'll tell you the bad news."

Br. Bede came back in a few minutes with the goodies, and prepared to tell the abbot what he didn't want to hear. This made him remember an old joke about how to break bad news:

A man who had been away from his family for a time, called his brother to find out how everyone was doing.

"How is my favorite cat, fluffy?" asked the first brother.

"Dead," said the second.

"Wow, that's cold, man," said the first brother. "It's cruel to break bad news so suddenly like that without softening me up for it first. You should have first said that the cat was on the roof and wouldn't come down, then said that you were putting a ladder up to save the cat. Then, that the cat fell off the roof. After that, I would have been better prepared for the bad news."

"Sorry," said the brother.

"Oh, that's OK," said the first brother. "I forgive you. By the way, how is mom?"

"Uh," replied the brother, "she's up on the roof."

Br. Bede chose to go a more direct route. "While you were gone, we had a small explosion in the kitchen, and as a result, Brother Canisius is at Detroit Receiving Hospital in a coma. Also, the kitchen is now unusable and we are unable to bake anything, let alone tarts. The one I gave you was baked a day before the explosion."

"Oh, my goodness," said Fr. Albert. "How did this happen?"

Bede told the whole story of Hunter Stephenson throwing a meat tenderizer at Br. Canisius' head, the missile missing its target by inches and the resultant gas line break and explosion.

"Has the boy who did this been arrested?" asked the abbot.

"No, father, he left amid the ruckus and hasn't been found yet. The police are looking for him, but so far, no luck."

"What is the prognosis for Brother Canisius?" he asked.

"Uncertain," said Br. Bede. "All of his vital signs are stable, but no one at Receiving seems able to say when, or even if, he will come out of his coma."

"OK," said Fr. Albert, "we'll visit him tomorrow and then look at what can be done to restore our kitchen…and our livelihood."

CHAPTER 28

After the others had left, Br. Philip knocked shyly on the door of Fr. Albert's chamber.

"Who is it?" barked the tired abbot.

"It is me, Brother Philip. May I come in?"

"OK, Philip," said Fr. Albert, "come in if you must."

Philip entered the abbot's sanctuary as Dorothy and her three companions had entered the great hall of the Wizard of Oz. Timidly, but with courageous purpose, Br. Philip announced that he had something to share with his abbot that he thought might help to soothe his troubled mind.

"Fine, Brother Philip, what balm have you brought to give me comfort?"

"My beloved abbot," said Br. Philip, "I was reading my Holy Bible, when I came across a scripture that should surely put your mind at ease.

Everything that has disquieted you was predicted by the prophet Isaiah. Listen to this, Father, it's awesome, it's from Isaiah, chapter 20:

>*Woe to those who call evil good, and good, evil, who change darkness into light, and light into darkness, who change bitter into sweet and sweet into bitter!*
>
>*Woe to those who are wise in their own sight, and prudent in their own esteem!*
>
>*Woe to the champions at drinking wine, the valiant at mixing strong drink!*
>
>*To those who acquit the guilty for bribes, and deprive the just man of his rights!*

"...and yada yada yada, the rest of the chapter is about the punishment they will receive. You know the routine: tongues of fire, earthquakes and corpses. I wouldn't want to be in their shoes for the world. So, you see, it's all part of the plan, you don't have to worry."

"Thank you, Brother Philip, I am familiar with the Book of Isaiah, but it was good of you to reacquaint me with those passages. You are right, it is all preordained, and I will take this as a gentle nudge from the Lord, through you of course, to chide me about letting the current condition of our world weigh so heavily upon my shoulders. Actually, I think it was sinful for me to assume responsibility for the whole of western society. God will care for His Creation; I will care for the monks of St. Adelaide Abbey. Thank you, Philip, you have done well."

Philip left the abbot's room and walked on clouds back to his own.

CHAPTER 29

The next day, Sarah Kessler came to work and Mrs. McNulty filled her in on all of the past week's drama. "I'm so sorry," she said.

"Don't worry," said Mrs. McNulty, "we take good care of each other around here, we'll be fine. By the way, I don't think you'll be seeing the likes of one Hunter Stephenson around here anytime soon. He's on the lamb and the cops can't find him."

"Wow," said Sarah, "I wonder if he will call me to turn himself in?"

"That's not his style, Ms. Kessler," said Mrs. McNulty.

At that point, Br. Philip walked in the door of the Guidance Center and saw the two women talking. "Am I interrupting anything?" he asked.

"Oh, look what the cat drug in," said Mrs.

McNulty.

"Um," he said, ignoring both the bait, and Mrs. McNulty, "I wonder if I could have a few moments of your time, Ms. Kessler?"

"I think that I could do that," she said. "Thanks to Mr. Stephenson, I have a whole hour free."

They went into Sarah's office and Br. Philip made himself as comfortable as one could while skating on such thin ice.

"What would you like to talk about?" she asked.

"Well," he started, "You heard about Brother Canisius, right?"

"Yes," she said, "I just heard from Mrs. McNulty, I hope that he gets better soon."

"Me too," said Br. Philip, "actually, I am having a pretty tough time about it. That, and Father Albert was missing, but he's back now. I don't know what to do."

"Brother Philip, are you asking me to take you on as a client? To help you work through your issues?"

Br. Philip never really thought about that. He considered it for a second or two. If he did that, he could see Sarah at least once a week. But then, if he became her client, there would be no chance of any other kind of relationship developing. No therapy then, he thought.

"No," he said, "That's not why I'm here." It was at this point that Br. Philip's previously joked-about, under-developed pre-frontal cortex failed him once again. He had learned in Psych 101 at U of D Mercy, that in most normal adult brains, the pre-frontal cortex handles many different functions, among which is the curtailment of impulses that might cause one to act in a capricious or foolish manner. Many have, at one time or another wanted to give the boss the finger or maybe flirt with someone else's spouse, but we don't. Somewhere in that pre-frontal cortex is a mechanism to check our behavior and keep us from doing something stupid. Br. Philip's professors have told him that the PFC is one of the last parts of our brains to fully develop, in some people not until they are in their mid to late twenties. That's why so many teenagers and young adults die young on jet-skis or get full-body tattoos of scenes from *Game of Thrones*. Br. Philip let it rip.

"I came here because I like you," he said, "and I wanted to see if I could give you a hug."

The moment unleashed a torrent of emotions in Br. Philip, each bouncing off of each other like a hive of frenzied bees. He felt elated that he had mustered the courage to cross this magic, invisible line. He felt a small sexual rush that he felt years ago before entering the monastery. He felt guilt. He felt danger. Anticipation. Lastly, he felt fear. Fear that he had once more made a fool of himself. Fear that she would say no. Fear that she would say yes.

Sarah had her own moment of uncertainty. Would that be unprofessional, she thought? An ethical violation? But then, he is not really a client, is he? More like a co-worker. Co-workers hug each other, she rationalized. Would this lead to an entanglement she was unprepared for? He's only asking for a hug, she thought, not a kiss. Was she attracted to him more than she had let on to herself?

"Alright, but just one," she said.

Br. Philip stood with an uneasy grin and held out his arms as if inviting both the Lady and the Tiger into his grasp. Sarah put her arms around him and gave him a rather chaste hug, not too much squeezing, heads far apart and careful with the bosom. Naturally, Br. Philip held on just a bit too long and Sarah found herself breaking the hug herself. Br. Philip, still residing on another planet, didn't notice the subtle hint.

"Thank you," he said, "I feel better already. May I have another?"

"No," said Sarah, "That was nice, but don't you need to get back to the abbey for chores or prayers?"

That stark reminder of who he really was, stung like a man whose mistress just showed him a picture of his wife and children.

"OK, thanks again for the hug, you're right, I do need to get back to the abbey," he said, as he crashed back to earth and then on to home.

CHAPTER 30

Hunter's new apartment was a stinking rathole in a part of the Cass Corridor that would never become gentrified. He knew that to avoid capture, he would need to live among people who don't care enough about you to call the police. He was unaccustomed to the roaches, rats and bedbugs who had lived there long before he did. Still, he thought, his current situation gave him some street cred that he never had before, with him coming from the suburbs and all. He began to feel a certain kinship, not so much with the homeless, but with the more interesting collection of criminals, anarchists and bohemians that lived in such surroundings.

Hunter shaved his head and grew a full beard which he dyed a shade of fuchsia likely never before seen on a human. He couldn't do anything about the snake/worm tattoo on his neck. He thought that his picture might be on display in the post office or on the law enforcement information network, so he didn't take any chances. Had his critical thinking skills been more developed, he would have known that the FBI, the Michigan State Police and the Detroit Police Department all had better things to do than launch a dragnet across the city to find Hunter Stephenson. He didn't know how long he could live like that, but he had enough money available to do it for a while. He bought himself a burner phone so that he could stay in contact with the few friends who would still speak to him. He remained angry at the world in general and the monks of St. Adelaide Abbey in particular. Why them? Why not? They were as good a focus for his anger as anyone, and it gave him faces to which he could attach his hatred.

While living in this new urban setting, Hunter gained access to several loosely affiliated anarchist groups in the area. The largest and most active of these was the Organization to Defeat Injustice in Urban Michigan or ODIUM. His new friends shared with Hunter a free-floating anger that could be directed toward almost any target deemed worthy of scorn. There were the usual subjects, of course: capitalism, religion, income inequality, racism, sexism, and myriad other isms. Police, brutality was the current focus of the group, but that target could change at any time in response to circumstances or trending issues. ODIUM's raison d'être was quite malleable as long as it involved righteous anger.

"How is the new crib working out bro?" The

man speaking was his new friend, Charles Gutierrez, head organizer for ODIUM. Charles used to be called Chuck, but these days he came to appreciate the prestige afforded by an unabridged first name. He felt that he was doing important work for the social justice movement and a childhood nickname just wouldn't do.

"It's a trip," said Hunter, "but I'm getting used to it. I met a few of my neighbors. I gave the old man downstairs a few bucks for groceries and he was very thankful. He also told me that my pink beard looked awesome. I'm still a little spooked by the rats, though. There aren't any in my apartment, but lots of them outside."

"Hang in there, man," said Charles, you'll get used to it.

CHAPTER 31

It was Br. Philip's turn to keep vigil at Br. Canisius hospital bed. He watched the gentle rising and falling of his brother's chest as he breathed, and realized that he loved Br. Canisius. Although Fr. Albert was the leader of the abbey, Br. Canisius was his mentor. Despite Br. Philip's immaturity and practical jokes, Br. Canisius had taken him under his wing and, over time, the two had grown close. Br. Philip noticed that Br. Canisius' lips seemed dry and chapped, so he walked over to the nurse's station and asked if he could feed him some ice-chips.

"Well," said the nurse, "we don't feed ice chips to a person in a coma, but thank you for noticing. I'll put some moisturizing balm on his lips."

"Thank you," said Br. Philip. "Also, do you think he could use an extra blanket? It seems a little cold in there."

"I appreciate your concern, Brother, but the temperature is just fine in his room, and we'll keep an eye on it. He is in no discomfort, I assure you."

Br. Philip went back into his friend's room and watched silently. He said a few prayers and asked God to bring Br. Canisius out of his coma. As he prayed, a nurse came into the room and announced "We have another visitor."

Br. Philip looked up to see who it was, and his heart dropped. When Sarah Kessler saw him, her face went red and she managed a mostly forced smile. "Brother Philip," she said, "I'm so sorry. I didn't know he already had a visitor. Do you mind if I stay?"

"No, Miss Kessler," he said, "I don't mind at all. Please come in."

"Miss Kessler?" she chided him. "I would think that we know each other well enough by now for you to call me Sarah. And besides, Mrs. McNulty is not here, so we can drop the formalities."

Once again, Br. Philip's emotions began to roil like an active volcano. After their last encounter, he felt that he had read her clearly, and that she was not interested in a romantic relationship with him. For that reason, he wished that he could vanish into the ether - or at least avoid looking at her face. On the other hand, he once again began to feel those magic butterflies of puppy-love flitting in his stomach. Man, this is complicated, he thought.

They discussed trivial things for a while and expressed their hopes for Br. Canisius to make a full recovery. There were several moments of dead air where neither Sarah nor Br. Philip could beget sufficient small talk. Finally, Sarah broke the ice.

"Philip, we both seem quite uncomfortable right now. We probably have some things to discuss and I'm getting a little hungry. What would you think if we were to get some lunch? It's on me."

The prospect of having lunch with the woman who had spurned his advances, thought Br. Philip, might be a torture equal to or worse than a Guantanamo prison waterboarding. Still, he said yes. He said yes because, buried somewhere beneath all of his embarrassment and shame, was a subconscious (yes, Freud was right about *some* things) spark of hope.

"I wish that I could," lied Br. Philip, "but we are keeping a vigil here for Br. Canisius, and I can't leave until my replacement arrives."

As if on cue, Brother Manuel entered the room. "Hello Sarah, Hello Br. Philip," he said, "relief has arrived!" For the second time in as many weeks, Br. Manuel heard the sound of Brahm's Lullaby and a sweet little glockenspiel.

"So," said Sarah to Br. Philip, "shall we then?"

CHAPTER 32

The abbey was quiet without the hustle and bustle from the kitchen. The monks continued to celebrate the Liturgy of the Hours, but with more sadness due to Br. Canisius' condition. They also had more time on their hands. There were no tarts to make, no bread runs or deliveries. The lack of work weighed heavily on all of the brothers but mostly on Fr. Albert and Br. Bede. The two assumed the responsibility for finding the money to replace the kitchen equipment and fix the structural damage caused by the explosion. There was no insurance because the abbey was self-indemnified and dependent on the Catholic Church for any extraneous funding needs. The Benedictines were different from other religious orders in that there was no central governing or funding body. Each monastery or abbey operated independently.

Br. Bede and Fr. Albert considered their options. Asking the Archdiocese or the Vatican for funding were bureaucratic bridges they would rather not cross. They considered setting up a GoFundMe page, but decided that the attitude toward Catholics on social media made that a risky proposition. They were out of ideas.

"I guess it's too late for a bake sale," quipped Fr. Albert.

"Or a garage sale," added Br. Bede. "We could turn the Tartmobile into a food truck and sell our tarts on the street."

The men were getting slap-happy because, in truth, they weren't sure the abbey would survive, and they didn't have a viable plan to move forward. Sometimes when things look bleakest, there is nothing to do but laugh.

As the two monks commiserated, Fr. Berthold appeared at the door with a stack of mail. He handed Fr. Albert the mail while lightly singing this little ditty: *"You'll wonder where the yellow went when you brush your teeth with Pepsodent."*

"Thank you, Father Berthold, for the mail," said Br. Bede, before turning to Fr. Albert to whisper, "I hope that I am as happy as that if I ever reach his age."

The mail contained the usual bills from fruit and sugar suppliers, newsletters from other monasteries, and one packet informing Fr. Albert that he "may already be a winner." At the bottom of the stack was a business size envelope addressed to *Sweet*

Marmalade Abbey c/o Father Albert Costello bearing no return address.

"Let me guess," said Br. Bede, "another offer for life insurance? A correspondence from a Nigerian prince with a deal you can't refuse?"

Fr. Albert opened the envelope and saw a check for $250,000. He chuckled and said, "You are right Bede, it's another scam of some sort. Before throwing it in the trash, however, he took a closer look. The check was not from an insurance or credit card company, it was from the bank account of Mrs. Grace Bommarito. He could not recall that he knew anyone with that name until he saw the short, hand-lettered note attached to the check.

> Dear Father Albert,
>
> I enjoyed our little chat at the Shrine. When I read about your misfortune last week, I thought that maybe I could help. Please feel free to use this money in any way that you see fit. Oh, and thanks again for letting me sit with you for a second time.
>
> Grace

"Who the heck is that?" asked Br. Bede

"That's the strange old lady I told you about that I met at the Shrine of the Cross in the Woods. Either she is as crazy as I thought she was, or she is both rich and generous. Let's find out which it is."

CHAPTER 33

Agroup of people, mostly men, sat around a table in the basement of Charles Gutierrez's apartment building. They were looking at videos of how to make a small but powerful bomb. Hunter was there, as were several people he did not know or recognize. Hunter had expressed to Charles an interest in learning how to make bombs. Charles trusted Hunter enough by now to have invited him to this meeting. As the men watched the videos and made comments or suggestions, a pipe was passed around the room. Charles noticed that of all the members present, Hunter seemed to be taking the most hits off of the pipe. He was high nearly all of the time now. And angry. He had outbursts even among his friends and he was frequently admonished to "chill."

All present, were members of ODIUM who

believed that they needed to take things to the next level if they ever wanted to make an impact for social justice. At the present time, they had no specific plans to use a bomb, but they wanted to have it available if needed. Besides, knowing that they *could* build one made them feel powerful.

"If I had it my way, I'd bomb those f---ing monks at St. Adelaide," Hunter announced to his comrades.

"Would you please," asked Charles, "just lay off those monks for a while? What did they ever do to hurt you or anyone else? I'm not interested in your personal crusades; we have bigger fish to fry."

Hunter's face remained petrous, but he was roiling inside. To be dressed down in front of his new friends was humiliating, but he said nothing. The group was important to him. Under the aegis of ODIUM he felt powerful and knew that ultimately they would have his back. He took another long hit off of the pipe, and withdrew to an old sofa in the corner of the room. He didn't care much about what transpired after that.

When the meeting was over, Hunter left without saying a word. On his way out, he pocketed a fancy Parker ballpoint pen that someone had left on the table.

CHAPTER 34

They found a popular little diner just off of Woodward Ave. The eatery was packed with a lunch crowd mainly consisting of staff from the nearby Detroit Medical Center and other Mid-town businesses. They were lucky to find a nice table in a corner. Many of the patrons stared at the black-robed monk who was clearly having lunch with an attractive young lady. And, they were drinking wine. They made for a most curious couple.

After a sip of her Pinot Grigio, Sarah spoke first. "Brother Philip, I like you very much..."

Br. Philip's heart jumped.

"...but we need to talk about the nature of our relationship. I think that maybe, under different circumstances, we could be more than just friends, but not right now. You have made a profound commitment to God and to your brothers at the abbey. Honestly, I would feel uncomfortable dating a monk, because I know that you are not supposed to date women – or anyone for that matter. And please, please, don't even consider the possibility of leaving the order so that you can be with me. If you did, I would feel even worse for being responsible for you breaking your vows."

Tears were beginning to well up in Br, Philip's eyes, but he choked them back. Sarah watched silently as he tried to compose himself. He remained unable to speak for a few moments and then, asked her "What am I supposed to do now?"

It wasn't an accusatory question. He knew that he could not blame Sarah for his own quixotic quest gone wrong. He knew that she was right. It was more like he was just thinking out loud. Before Sarah could answer him, Philip's face went through a sudden metamorphosis. His look of shock and despair was replaced with one of gentle confidence. He said it again, but this time with a smile, and a conciliatory shrug of his shoulders, "What am I supposed to do now?"

"Eat your burger," said Sarah. And he did.

Br. Philip's mood had lifted almost immediately. One minute ago, he was ready to shed tears, but now, through the grace of God, he felt gratitude for the clarity of his situation. A weight had been lifted from his shoulders. He smiled.

"Sarah, thank you for being brave enough to tell me what I needed to hear. I've been acting like an ass and you put a mirror up to my face. Tonight, I will thank God for sending me a lovely Jewish siren

– and then keeping me from bashing myself into the rocks."

Sarah laughed. "I've never been called a siren before, but I guess it is not the worst thing a man has ever said to me. In fact, I kind of like it. I'll take it. I'll be your siren."

The remainder of the lunch was surprisingly enjoyable for both of them. Gone was the sexual tension of two people who were uncertain about each other. Gone was the discomfort between the jilted and the jilter. The newly forged relationship felt like a good fit for Sarah and for Br. Philip. They joked with each other and reveled in this new amicability. They had a second glass of wine, and said goodbye. There were no hugs or requests for hugs. Br. Philip, however, knew that he had some more work to do with his soul.

CHAPTER 35

Br. Bede did a Google search on the name Grace Bommarito. It didn't take him long to find out that she was the real thing. She was the heiress to a fortune built on supplying parts to the Big Three and other automobile manufacturers. She was the only child of Nina and Benedetto Censoplano, a man known in the Motor City as Big Ben. When he died in 1990, Grace took over as CEO of the company and used her wealth for many philanthropic causes throughout southeast Michigan. Because Big Ben had inherited the family business from his own father, Grace was considered "old money," and lived in the traditional suburb of Grosse Pointe Shores. She married another rich Detroiter named Vincent Bommarito and when he died last year, she also inherited most of his wealth.

Br. Bede rushed to tell Fr. Albert the news: the check was legit. The staid Fr. Albert rose up from his Eames lounge chair and launched into a spirited dance of joy. His smile told the story. He was elated.

"You know, Brother Bede, I have been deeply and genuinely happy since the day I got back from The Cross in the Woods. I had been down in the dumps about the state of post-Christian America, and I was letting it weigh on my shoulders like a millstone. You won't believe who started to bring me out of my funk. Go ahead, Bede, take a guess."

"I truly have no idea, Abbot," said Br. Bede.

"OK," said Fr. Albert. "It was Brother Philip of all people!"

"Tell me more, Father" said an incredulous Br. Bede.

"I certainly will," said the Abbot. "The day I came back, after finding out about the explosion and meeting with you, I had a brief visit from Brother Philip. He had been concerned about my mental state and said that he found a scripture that he thought might help me. Brother Bede, I don't know if you are aware of this, but Brother Philip has a first-class mind. Despite his shortcomings, of which we are both quite aware, he is a very smart man. Anyway, he read to me a few verses from Isaiah 5:20…"

"Ah," said Br. Bede, interrupting the Abbot, "Woe to those who call evil good, and good, evil, who change darkness into light, and light into darkness, who change bitter into sweet and sweet into bitter!"

"Yes, very good Brother Bede, he said. "We both know the chapter well, but for some reason this time it meant much more to me than it had in the past. It felt very personal. Brother Philip was trying to show me that I had no business getting upset about worldly things when all of this has been pre-ordained by God and spoken through the prophets. Philip was right, of course, the current state of Western civilization is none of my business; other than to minister to the men and women who are suffering from it. One of my favorite writers, Thomas Merton, the Trappist monk, once described the morgue at Bellevue Hospital as 'a place where they collect the bodies of those who died of contemporary civilization.'"

Br. Bede laughed. "Father Albert, I am so happy to see you smiling again. If it is OK with you, I would like to make arrangements for us to visit with Mrs. Bommarito so that we may thank her in person. After all, a quarter of a million dollars deserves more than a simple thank you note."

"By all means, Brother Bede, invite her over for dinner." He then remembered that the abbey no longer had a kitchen in which to prepare such a dinner. "Oh wait," he said, "better to take her out to dinner somewhere nice."

"I'll take care of it right away," said Br. Bede.

CHAPTER 36

Hunter sat in a threadbare recliner in his apartment building while repeatedly throwing his knife at an old bookcase. It didn't matter to him that it was a furnished apartment and he did not own the bookcase. The blade rarely stuck into the wood, but when it did, he gave it a name. "Gotcha Dad, how does that feel? This one's for you, Brother Canisius, you lying roadie. Sarah, yeah baby, right between the eyes! Counsel this. Charles, who died and made you king of ODIUM? "Assholes one and all," he said.

There was a knock on his door and he answered it with the knife still in his hand. It was the elderly downstairs neighbor to whom he had given money to buy food. The man was slight of build and stooped over from age and misery. He appeared to be Hispanic, and held a well-worn woolen cap in his hand. "I'm so sorry, Hunter," the man said timidly in broken English, "I hate to ask, but would you mind please keeping it down a little? All that thumping is giving me a headache."

"If you don't get lost and leave me alone," growled Hunter, "I'll give you a headache you'll never forget. Now go, old man!"

The man left, and Hunter returned to his knife-tossing. "Boom," he said, "big man Bede. Let's see how tough you are with a knife in your belly!" He ruminated about all of his recent humiliations like a cow chewing its cud. Bring it up. Chew on it for a while. Swallow it. Repeat.

Clearly, Hunter Stephenson's young life was coursing on a downward arc. The list of people for whom Hunter harbored anger, seemed of late, to grow exponentially. His new social circle left a lot to be desired, and at times, having so many angry people together only fueled the demons of his soul. He and his comrades rationalized their anti-social behavior as being justified because they were fighting for a good cause, but it was obvious that, like Hunter, their motivations came more from an angry place, than from a desire to help. Tearing down the system could give one a great feeling of power.

Hunter tossed the knife a few more times and then put it away. He lit up a joint. "My best friend" he said.

CHAPTER 37

When Br. Philip returned to St. Adelaide, the abbey was eerily quiet. There were no sounds coming from the burned-out kitchen, and he learned that Br. Bede and Fr. Albert had gone out on some sort of errand. With Br. Canisius in the hospital and Br. Manuel holding vigil there, only a skeleton crew held fort at the abbey. Br. Philip decided to pray alone in the oratory. It was daytime and the sun shone brightly through the stained-glass windows, painting the room with a kaleidoscopic luminance. In the silence, Br. Philip could hear the gentle ticking of a nearby clock, one of his favorite sounds. His senses took it all in: the colors, the sounds, the smell of candles and freshly polished wood. It was glorious. He prayed there for over two hours. He prayed for Br. Canisius' recovery, for the funding to repair the kitchen, and he prayed that Hunter, the man who had caused the damage, would find grace in Jesus. Mostly, however, he said prayers of thanks for the blessings he had received recently. After his lunch with Sarah, he enjoyed a clarity of purpose unlike anything he had experienced since taking his vows.

Looking around the oratory, Br. Philip remembered that this was where he had played that marmalade prank on Br. Canisius. That seemed so childish now. Was he still that person? He didn't think so, and wished that he could take it all back now. But he would not dwell on past mistakes and shortcomings. Right now, he felt new. He felt like a real monk, or at least what he thought a real monk should feel like.

Br. Philip's reverie was broken by a loud crashing sound coming from just outside the vestibule. He ran out of the chapel to find Fr. Berthold lying on the floor with shards of a bone-china teacup scattered about him. He had apparently fallen while walking precariously with a cup of tea. He was conscious but, judging from his moans, in obvious pain.

"Father," cried Br. Philip, "what happened? Are you OK?"

The old priest looked up at him and said, 'Timex. Takes a lickin' and keeps on tickin'."

"Can you stand up? Br Philip asked, while offering his arm for support. Fr. Berthold attempted to rise, but instead cried out in pain.

"Stay where you are Father and don't try to move," said Br. Philip, "I'm calling for an ambulance."

CHAPTER 38

Br. Bede drove the Tartmobile down Lake Shore Road while Fr. Albert rode shotgun looking for the address of Grace Bommarito's home. The drive down Lake Shore was among the most beautiful to be found in the Detroit area. On one side of the road was picturesque Lake St. Clair with its deep blue water accented by ever shimmering whitecaps. On the other side, stood the elegant mansions of the old families that made Detroit what it once was. There were grand Tudor homes rising up from large well-manicured lawns. Sprawling Cotswold manors sat next to contemporary multi-million-dollar homes. The owners of these great houses had one thing in common: they were rich.

Br. Bede found it ironic that wealth could buy such beauty. "Man," he said to Fr. Albert, "we sure don't get out to this neck of the woods very often, do we?"

"No we don't," answered the Abbot, "there is a beautiful view out of any window in the car."

They eventually found the address and motored up a long asphalt driveway through an esplanade of neatly trimmed hedgerows punctuated with a colonnade of grand stone posts. It was breathtaking. They were met at the door by Mrs. Bommarito herself, who ushered them into a large room with comfortable, not ostentatious, furniture. "Would you like some coffee or tea?" she asked.

"I would love a cup of coffee, Mrs. Bommarito," said Br. Bede.

"Tea for me, please," followed Fr. Albert.

She left to get the drinks and the two men looked around the room. "Look," said Fr. Albert, pointing, "she has a nice carved wood crucifix on the wall."

"And a framed picture of *Our Mother of Perpetual Help* over there," added Br. Bede. "I guess she's one of us. Thank God."

Although she did have ample paid staff (she still referred to them as her servants), Grace Bommarito liked to do things herself whenever it was possible. After a few minutes, she returned with a tray of coffee, tea and a half-dozen fresh cannoli. Fr. Albert's eyes lit up. "I haven't had one of those in years!"

"Mrs. Bommarito," said Br. Bede, thank you for inviting us over. Your donation was so generous that we wanted to meet you so that we could thank you in person. You don't know how much this means to us."

"Oh, I think I have some idea," she replied. "When I read about your explosion, it reminded me of the day I met Fr. Albert up in Indian River. He is such a nice man. I knew that God had put the two of us together for a reason, but I didn't know what it was. Now I do."

"I don't know how we can ever thank you, Mrs. Bommarito," said Fr. Albert.

"I'll tell you how," she said. "When you get that kitchen of yours up and running again, I want first crack at a batch of your lemon-marmalade tarts. If you do that, I'll consider us even."

"I'll tell you what," said Br. Bede, "we'll do you one better. We will throw in a box of our famous Bakewell tarts as well."

"Deal," said Mrs. Bommarito. "But wait. There is one more thing you can do for me. I think you guys have a special connection to the man upstairs, if you know what I mean, so if you would be so kind, would you please say a special prayer for my niece? Her son has gotten himself into some kind of trouble and now he has disappeared. No one has seen him for weeks and my niece is brokenhearted."

"We would be happy to pray for your niece and her son, said Fr. Albert. What are their names?"

"My niece is Carol and her son's name is Hunter."

The men went silent and looked at each other for a cue as to what to say next. Br. Bede took the lead. "Mrs. Bommarito, I don't want to pry, but is Hunter's last name Stephenson?"

"Yes, it is. How on earth did you know that?" she asked.

"Well," said Fr. Albert, "I don't' know how to tell you this, but Hunter Stephenson is the man who blew up our kitchen. And we don't know where he is either."

"Good heavens!" she cried. "I guess the Lord brought us together for more than one purpose. Will you pray for all of us then?"

"Yes, we will," they said in unison. The monks left Mrs. Bommarito with two grateful hugs and a blessing from the Abbot.

CHAPTER 39

Fr. Berthold was taken by EMS to Detroit Receiving hospital where the doctors quickly diagnosed a broken hip and a probable concussion. Br. Philip sat in the waiting room while various physicians and nurses employed pain medication and surgery to stabilize the old priest's hip. Later, Doctor Kumar told Br. Philip that he used a combination of pins, rods and screws to put the old monk's hip back together.

"Kind of like an Erector set?" asked Br. Philip.

"Yes," said the doctor, "he will be immobilized for quite some time. I have to tell you that a hip fracture in a patient this old is a serious matter. It may never heal completely and in the elderly, it often marks the begin of a downward turn in general health. We can wish for the best but I wouldn't want to give you false optimism."

"Thank you for your honesty Doctor Kumar," said Br. Philip. "When will I be able to see him?"

"He is in the recovery room right now, but as soon as he is moved to a regular room someone will come down to get you. It shouldn't be too long. By the way, we are also concerned about his cognitive state. We believe he had a concussion in the fall, but we won't know for sure until more tests are done. He also said some things that hinted at delirium. For example, before the surgery, we explained to him what we were going to do and he said 'See the USA in your Chevrolet.' Also, when he first arrived in the Emergency Room, despite being in great pain, he told the ER nurse, 'It's Miller Time!'"

Br. Philip laughed. "That is not delirium, doctor," he said, "that is Father Berthold. I'm afraid that he has been like that for a long time. He never gets better, never gets worse. We got used to it eventually and, to be honest, we now find it quite endearing."

The waiting room was a microcosm of humanity. The quiet ones buried their faces in magazines or fiddled with their smart phones. The nervous ones couldn't stay seated for more than a couple minutes and paced the floor. The gregarious ones struck up conversations with their neighbors. One older woman just stared at people and maintained a carefully cultivated scowl on her face. When she looked at Br. Philip, he smiled and waved at her. In response, she too buried her face in a *People* magazine.

Br. Philip tried reading the well-worn copy of today's *Detroit News,* but found he couldn't concentrate. He prayed silently for a while, but couldn't concentrate on that either. It was difficult when two of his friends and brothers were in such conditions and he could do nothing to help. Then he remembered what he had said to Fr. Albert about not worrying about things you could not control. He felt better. "Thank you, Lord," he said under his breath.

After about an hour, a friendly nurse walked into the waiting room, looked around and headed in Br. Philip's direction. "Let me guess," he said, "you must be Brother Philip."

"How did you guess?" asked Br. Philip. "Was it the black robe and rosary? Am I the only one dressed like this?"

"You got it," he said. "My name is Kevin, and if you'll come with me, I'll take you to see your friend Father Berthold. He is awake now."

He followed Kevin up to the third floor and down several labyrinthian hallways. They stopped at room 324. Br. Philip was familiar with the room.

"Hey, did they put him in the same room as Brother Canisius?" he asked.

"Yes, said Kevin, "we thought that it would be more convenient for all of you ceaseless warriors. One stop shopping for the men in black."

Br. Philip entered the room and said hello to Br. Manuel who was holding vigil for Br. Canisius. He made a sign of the cross for Br. Canisius before heading past him to Fr. Berthold's bed. Fr. Berthold looked up at him and smiled.

Br. Philip smiled back and asked him how he was feeling.

"Not too good," he replied.

"Did you know," asked Br. Philip, "that you are roommates with Br. Canisius?"

"Who?"

"Brother Canisius. Remember, he came here after the explosion, and he's still in a coma."

"Coma, coma, coma chameleon," said Fr. Berthold.

After a little more superficial chit-chat with the father, Br. Philip went over to talk to Br. Manuel. "How is he doing?" he asked.

"No change," said Br. Manuel, "but at least he's not getting worse. The doctor said that if he doesn't show signs of improvement soon, they will have to transfer him to a long-term-care facility."

"All we can do is pray," said Br. Philip.

"You are right, brother," said Br. Manuel. "By the way," he added, "did you eat an orange while you were waiting?"

"Yes, how did you know"

"Jimmy Buffet told me. The minute you walked in the room, I was *Wasting Away in Margaritaville*."

CHAPTER 40

On their way back from Mrs. Bommarito's mansion, Br. Bede and Fr. Albert decided to swing by the Avalon Bakery and pick up some bread. Carla greeted them at the door, as cheerful as ever.

"What are you so happy about, Carla?" asked Br. Bede. "Oh, wait," he added "you don't need a reason. You're always happy, my friend."

"Hello Brother Bede," she said, grinning ear to ear, "and Father Albert, the Abbot, his-own-self, what brings you to this part of town?"

"Well, naturally," said the Abbot, "we came to pick up a big load of the best bread in town. And also, to share our good news. You see, a donor who wishes to remain anonymous has given the abbey a very large sum of money – enough for us to restore and modernize the kitchen. We'll be back in business in no time. It is quite the blessing."

"Praise the Lord," said Carla, "no one deserves it more than you brothers do. I'm so happy for you."

"Thank you," said Fr. Abbot.

"I might be getting some good news myself soon," said Carla, "if the Lord wills it. We have a good profit-sharing plan at this bakery, and I have been here so long that the bosses say they might make me a part owner!" she beamed.

"Fantastic," said Br. Bede.

"Good work, Carla," added Fr. Albert. "Was it our Bakewell tarts that moved you to the top?" he asked.

"That, and the good Lord Jesus," she said, "Hallelujah. But it's not a done deal yet," she cautioned. "They'll let me know in a week or so."

"We'll say some prayers for you," said the two monks in unison.

On the ride back to St. Adelaide Abbey, Fr. Albert commented, "I think that Carla just might be the best witness for Christ that I have ever known."

"Amen, brother," said Br. Bede.

CHAPTER 41

The men and women of ODIUM were meeting again in the basement of Charles Gutierrez. A seasoned anarchist from Seattle, Washington known only by the nom de' guerre "Territ Down," was there to provide inspiration and technical direction to the group. He had been an integral part of the takeover of private and government property for the purpose of creating an "autonomous zone" during the 2020 riots over police brutality. Hunter listened quietly as Mr. Down encouraged the group to do something more dramatic if they wanted to establish a name for themselves and gain the respect of their oppressors. The group discussed various options including a takeover of Detroit Police Headquarters, sabotage of the water treatment plant, occupation of the new

Jeep factory and the bombing of any iconic building in the city.

Ultimately, ODIUM was not sure it had the endorsement of enough people in Detroit to carry off a major occupation or takeover. That would take more soldiers than they had. Also, the Detroit Police Department of late had greater support from the populace than Seattle's force had enjoyed. They switched their discussion to setting off a bomb somewhere. But which icon would give them the most bang for the buck, so to speak? Ford Field? That was the symbol of capitalist power in the Motor City. Little Caesar's Arena? Who did the Ilitch family think they were? The Spirit of Detroit statue? It was guarded too closely now since the vandalism that was inflicted by Hunter and his friends. The Belle Isle Bridge? That would take more technical expertise than they currently possessed.

Hunter suggested that they blow up the St. Adelaide Abbey. Charles gave him a look that he understood immediately.

Territ Down, being a man of experience, had a suggestion of his own. "Look, folks," he said, 'you want to make a point but you don't want to get yourselves killed. You need a target that will allow you easy access with minimal risk. In Seattle, we have had a great deal of luck targeting the gentry. These scumbags come into rundown but otherwise desirable areas, throw all the poor people, most of whom are minorities, out on their assess, and then they move back in to their upper-class paradise. It's sickening.

The gentry. Rich people. Others in the group warmed to the idea and soon all knew where they would strike. The heavily gentrified Midtown area (nee: The Cass Corridor).

CHAPTER 42

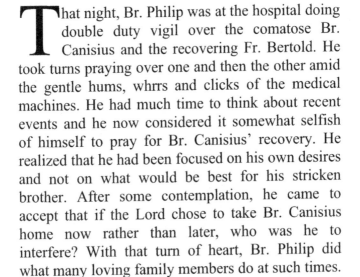

That night, Br. Philip was at the hospital doing double duty vigil over the comatose Br. Canisius and the recovering Fr. Bertold. He took turns praying over one and then the other amid the gentle hums, whrrs and clicks of the medical machines. He had much time to think about recent events and he now considered it somewhat selfish of himself to pray for Br. Canisius' recovery. He realized that he had been focused on his own desires and not on what would be best for his stricken brother. After some contemplation, he came to accept that if the Lord chose to take Br. Canisius home now rather than later, who was he to interfere? With that turn of heart, Br. Philip did what many loving family members do at such times. He leaned in close to Br. Canisius face and whispered, "Brother, it's OK for you to let go if you are ready to meet our Father. I will let go of you myself if it is God's will."

With that, Br. Philip did indeed pray for God's will in whatever form it should take. He heard a light moan coming from Fr. Bertold's side of the room and he went over to see how the old man was faring.

"Father Bertold," said Br. Philip, "how are you doing? Are you in any pain?"

"I heard you praying over Br. Canisius," he said. "Remember, son, 'there is a time to be born and a time to die'."

"Yes Father, Ecclesiastes," said Br. Philip. "Thank you for helping me keep things in perspective. Maybe it is his time to go. I can accept that now." Philip was impressed that Fr. Berthold seemed so lucid, until…

"Hope I die before I get old," said Fr. Berthod.

"I think it's a little too late for that," quipped Br. Philip.

He stayed for another hour until he was relieved by Br. Bede.

"How are they doing?' asked Br. Bede.

"No change in Brother Canisius that I can see. Father Berthold is still in some pain, and his mental state is, like always: up and down, or should I say in and out? By the way, Brother Bede," said Br. Philip, "I have been doing some thinking. I would love to see Brother Canisius make it out of this, but I have come to terms with the possibility that he will not. If that happens, I think now, that I can accept it as being OK."

"Good," said Br. Bede. "You have grown deeply

in the past few months, both personally and spiritually. You should know that I am proud to be your brother."

CHAPTER 43

That evening, back at the abbey during Vespers, Mrs. McNulty summoned Br. Philip to come to the office.

"I'm sorry to disturb your service, Brother Phillip," she said, "but Brother Bede is on the phone from the hospital and he said that he needs to speak to you right away. It doesn't sound like good news."

When Br. Philip put the receiver to his ear, he heard the news that he had been expecting.

"Brother Philip," said Br. Bede in somber tones, "I am sorry to tell you that we have lost a brother tonight."

"I sort of expected this," said Br. Philip. "When did Brother Canisius pass away?"

"Wait Brother, listen," said Br. Bede, "it was not Brother Canisius who died, it was Father Berthold."

"What?" cried Br. Philip. I just saw him a few

hours ago and he looked fine"

"I know," said Br. Bede, "it was the strangest thing. He closed his eyes as if to sleep and never re-opened them. He gave a long and gentle sigh, and then, just died."

"Requiescat in pace," said Br. Philip. He felt a twinge of guilt when he realized his relief that it wasn't his good friend Br. Canisius. "OK, Brother, thanks for letting us know," he said, "I'll tell the others."

"Wait," said Br. Bede, "there's more. At the moment of Fr. Berthold's passing, I heard some rustling from the other bed. Brother Canisius had awakened. He has asked that you come and see him as soon as you can."

"I'll be right there," said Br. Philip.

CHAPTER 44

Though it was the middle of the night, Br. Philip and Fr. Albert drove through the darkness to visit their newly re-animated brother. When they arrived, they found Br. Canisius sitting up in his bed, his face bearing a triumphant grin. Without even saying hello, he said, "Brother Bede has told me all about it. I guess I was knocked out from an explosion that I do not remember at all, and I have been in a coma for weeks. I don't know why God chose to bring me back at this hour, but I am grateful that He has. Does anyone have a Bakewell tart handy? I'm starving."

The four monks laughed, exchanged hugs and said a prayer of thanks for what God had done.

"We hope to see you back at the abbey as soon as possible" said Fr. Albert. "We're running out of candles and if you don't come back soon, we'll be plunged into darkness."

"Why didn't you just buy some? Asked Br. Canisius.

"Well," said Br. Philip, "if we had done that, we wouldn't have been able to play the victim card and blame you!"

Br. Canisius laughed. "Same old Philip," he said, "always the jokester."

"That is where you are wrong," said Br. Bede. "Brother Philip is actually a very different man these days. He has grown very much in his spiritual walk, and I think that you will find the new Brother Philip to be an inspiration to be around.

As they were talking, a hospital transporter came in with a gurney. I'll need to close this curtain around you while I remove your roommate from the room.

"Wait," said Fr. Albert. We are all brothers here and we would prefer that you leave the curtain open as you take our brother away."

"Our brother?" said a confused Br. Canisius. "Who is it."

As the attendants wheeled the body of Br. Berthold out of the room, the monks each made a sign of the cross. Br. Bede took the lead in breaking the news to Br. Canisius. He filled him in with all of the details about the Father falling and breaking his hip, as well as his seemingly good disposition up until the end. Finally, Br. Bede told Br. Canisius that mere seconds had passed between Fr. Berthold's death and Br. Canisius' own re-awakening.

"I have no words," said Br. Canisius.

CHAPTER 45

Work on the new kitchen was progressing very well, as was the health of Br. Canisius. His mind was as sharp as ever but he was still weak from the significant weight-loss he suffered during his coma. Br. Philip made it a point to help his good friend recover as quickly as possible. He even agreed to let Br. Canisius teach him the art of candle-making so that there would always be someone in the abbey who knew how to keep the light burning.

Fr. Albert reveled in his new found distance from the cares of the world. He even began jokingly referring to life outside of the abbey as that of "the English" as the Amish always called the outside world. When a recent boisterous protest by ODIUM and some other anarchist groups resulted in damaged buildings and an overturned police car, the

Abbot said simply, "The English are at it again. They could do well to learn gratitude and forgiveness."

One morning at breakfast Br. Bede was feeling particularly sad about the passing of Fr. Berthold. As a tear ran down his cheek, he said, "I would give anything to hear one of Fr. Berthold's sayings again.

With that, Br. Philip cupped his hands together and said in a faux deep voice, "Don't worry Brother Bede...You're in good hands – with Allstate."

Br. Bede laughed and the mood of the entire group was immediately lightened. "Thank you, Brother Philip. I told you that you would become a great addition to St. Adelaide Abbey, and the proof is in the pudding."

"Is it Jello brand?" replied Br. Philip, and they laughed again.

A trip to the Avalon Bakery was planned for later in the day, but there was concern about the trip because a major demonstration had been planned for a protest over a police shooting. The march was to begin near Wayne State University and continue through the mid-town area right past the bakery.

A discussion was held and the men decided that as Christians, they could not avoid their duties out of a fear of the unknown. They would go to the Avalon as planned and secure the daily bread that they needed. To be safe, four of the men would go together this time: Brs. Bede, Philip, Canisius and Manuel. Fr. Albert would remain back at the abbey and pray for the safety of his charges.

CHAPTER 46

Hunter was excited about the demonstration. After his recent arrest and embarrassment, he needed a boost to make him feel important and part of something meaningful again. He didn't have to wait too long, as a black man named Demauntre Harris had been shot dead by Detroit police on Wednesday, and the word went out on social media that there would be a rally for justice on Friday near Wayne State University. Hunter ditched his plaid shirt and sneakers for a set of hard black boots, black denims and a black shirt. That, a can of pepper spray and a switchblade he bought on eBay would round out his ensemble. Serious protest gear. He also had a black pull-up facemask left over from the Covid-19 pandemic in his back pocket. He would wear it so as to remain anonymous if any trouble broke out.

The crowd was gathering at the corner of Cass Avenue and West Warren. Hunter enjoyed the fact that so many like-minded people came together to support Mr. Harris and protest police brutality. But the group appeared to have some difficulty staying on point. In addition to the police brutality protesters, there were signs promoting LGBTQ rights, people handing out climate change tracts, anti-war banners, and a general hodgepodge of anti-capitalist warriors. Hunter fed off the fervid energy like an evangelical minister in the heat of a revival meeting.

A woman with bare breasts approached him, holding a sign proclaiming that taking milk from cows was an obscene form of cultural appropriation. Though not a vegan, Hunter always appreciated the use of women's naked breasts to make a point. He spotted his friend Charles handing out water at one the ODIUM tents and went over to say hello. Charles gave him the super-secret handshake known only to the anointed ones and they shared a fresh, good-sized blunt.

"So, what's the deal?" asked Hunter. "What's goin' down?"

Charles filled him in on the particulars. "Same old story, man, another innocent black man gunned down by the police." Except, Charles pronounced it as the *PO-leece* even though he was not black. Hunter, in his more lucid moments knew that it was common practice for some white and Hispanic protestors to begin using the slang and word pronunciations of urban African Americans whenever the protest was about anything concerning black people. They believed that it bonded them with blacks and showed respect for black culture. Actually, most black people felt embarrassed for them or annoyed when white liberals lapsed into blackspeak.

The crowd began to move up West Warren Avenue toward Cass as Hunter joined the queue. Someone handed him a sign proclaiming NO JUSTICE NO PEACE, and Hunter held it solemnly above his head like a processional cross carried by an altar boy. He was doing his part. Next to him was a young man of middle-eastern appearance who handed out coupons for fifty-percent-off a sandwich at his father's convenience store. The bare-breasted woman bounced along four rows behind Hunter. All told, it appeared that the ethnic make-up of the crowd was about sixty/forty in favor of white people.

The demonstration edged forward for a few blocks and then turned right on Cass Avenue where they were met with a small group of counter protesters. This group waved American flags and many wore the red *Make America Great Hats* that served as lightning rods for the leftist groups. The appearance of that second group made it much more likely that the most intolerant and volatile personalities on both the left and right would soon have their day. They would each be able to express the righteous anger and indignation to which only their side had rights. As the angry factions glared at each other a young white boy of about five years of age, broke ranks with his mother and reached out to hand some dandelions to a black girl of about the same age. The girl smiled and accepted the gift. The boy's mother snatched him back with fear in her eyes.

A young woman with spiked pink hair marching next to Hunter looked him gravely in the eyes and said, "You know, this whole thing is really about feminism and the oppression of women."

"How so?" asked Hunter, seeking some clarification on a connection he had not yet made.

"Because police brutality is all about the abuse of power by men and no one has been abused by powerful men more than women," she said.

"OK," said Hunter, "good luck."

At that point, a black man walking behind them interjected. "Hey sweetheart, don't make this about you 'cause it ain't about you. You ain't the victim here, Demauntre Harris is the victim."

Nearby, a thin man wearing a flamboyant rainbow chiffon scarf begged to differ. He was about to give his own two cents on who wins the victimhood sweepstakes when he was drowned out by a short mustachioed man with a megaphone who was dressed so as to bear a remarkable resemblance to the Monopoly Man. "Down with corporate America," he barked "down with capitalist pigs!"

One sign proclaimed in capital letters:

WE DON'T ASK FOR JUSTICE, WE DEMAND IT

WE WILL NEVER FORGET OR FORGIVE

WE HAVE THE POWER AND WE WILL GET MORE

Hunter read the sign and thought back to his conversation with Br. Philip. The one about humility forgiveness and gratitude.

CHAPTER 47

Four blocks south of the march, Carla watched the peloton inch closer to the Avalon Bakery. While she abhorred police brutality, she had concerns about the veracity of this particular brutality charge.

Mr. Harris, it seemed, was a career criminal who had been confronted by police with the proceeds of a recent local robbery in his possession. The police had decided to take him in for questioning and were attempting to put handcuffs on his wrists when he began to struggle with the officers.

Here is where the story got murky. Police said that Harris attempted to grab the gun of a young black female officer when he was shot by another. Word on the street spread quickly that Demauntre was unarmed and was shot by a white officer. Speaking on local television news, the police chief said that it was unclear which officer had fired the shot, but most likely it was the seasoned black officer and that it was a justified shooting. Carla would never have joined such a protest without clear evidence of culpability.

As Carla watched the approaching marchers, Brs. Philip and Bede arrived for the scheduled bread purchase. "Hey, Carla," said Br. Philip, "looks like we have some excitement coming our way."

"That's fine with me," said Carla, "as long as we don't have no brick throwin' or burnin' down buildings. I got promoted last week, and now I am a part owner of this place. It's the best place I ever worked, and the best thing that's ever happened to me. Ain't nobody gonna burn this place down."

Br. Philip assured Carla that nobody would damage the bakery today, and then loaded his dolly with bread that she had gathered for him. He noticed that there were four more loaves than Br. Manuel had ordered. He thought about saying nothing, but then yelled "Hey Carla, you gave us too much!"

Carla smiled and said, "Keep it, brother, it's a tip."

Down the street, the demonstrators continued moving south toward West Willis Street, closer to the Avalon Bakery. Carla hoped that they would keep going straight on Cass and not turn right onto West Willis. They turned right.

The group marched relentlessly down West Willis like Rommel into Africa. Carla turned to Br. Bede and asked him if he could protect the bakery from the invaders. He said that he would try. As the group of angry protesters inched ever closer to the bakery, Br. Canisius spotted a familiar face among the crowd. One man with a bald head and a technicolor beard had a face that looked vaguely familiar. A few synapses in Br. Canisius' brain fired before he made the connection. The man had a feeble tattoo of a snake on his neck that looked more like an earthworm. That was him. The face of the bald, vibrantly bearded character was that of Hunter Stephenson – the man who had put him into the hospital. That man was screaming loudly and holding a sign with an obscene slogan about authority figures in general.

The entourage shouted prefabricated slogans as they marched down West Willis. "Justice for Demauntre," they yelled. "Defund the Police," they cried. "End systemic racism," they intoned. "Liberation for LGBTQs," said another. Any fair observer could see that the myriad causes of the heterogenous group would belie any sense of unity among the perpetually offended.

As the group of protestors edged closer to the Avalon Bakery, Br. Bede stiffened. His years as a bouncer had given him a sharpened sense of impending danger. The fight or flight response remained acute in him, and he steeled himself to the possibility of having to act, should the situation require such a response.

Br. Canisius said to Br. Bede, "I think I just saw Hunter Stephenson."

"No," said Br. Bede, "I don't see him."

Br. Canisius pointed to the man in black with a shaved head and a fuchsia beard.

"That's him," he said, "I remember that face. Ignore the bald head and the pink or purple beard, and that's him. See, he has a snake tattoo on his neck. That's Hunter Stephenson. I'm sure of it,"

Br. Bede gave the man a second look. "You are right, Brother Canisius, that is him. I see the worm on his neck. I'll make him forget that he ever set foot in St. Adelaide Abbey," said Br. Bede

"No, please," begged Br. Canisius, "we must forgive him. It is what Jesus would do."

"Yes," added Br. Philip, "please do not hurt him."

CHAPTER 48

As the group of protestors advanced down West Willis Avenue, the anger of the assemblage stiffened. Having a Ph.D. in psychology, Br. Bede knew that mobs, as a rule, start out as a collection of like-minded individuals united by one purpose, and then devolve into an anonymous mass of mindless automatons driven by emotion, untethered to reason. Some picked up rocks and hurled them into the windows of gentrified apartments and storefronts. Others threw rocks aimlessly. Shattered windows fell like glitter confetti onto the sidewalks. Other marchers directed their anger at the counter-protestors lining the parade route. In any event, the initial purpose of the protest was now clearly lost. It was simply a riot.

Both Br. Canisius and Br. Bede watched Hunter Stephenson advance on the bakery. He held something in his hand, something that looked to Br. Bede to be suspicious. He was the first to notice that it looked like a bomb. Hunter was now no more than fifty feet from the Avalon Bakery. Br. Bede, his bouncer instincts kicking into play, lunged into action and before Hunter could react, smashed a meaty fist into the young anarchist's face, knocking him out cold. The crudely made bomb fell to the pavement and fizzled out in an impotent denouement.

"Brother Bede, you hit him!" cried Br. Canisius. "Remember that you are a man of the cloth."

"I'm sorry brother, but I didn't hit him out of anger," said Br. Bede, "I hit him to save lives. Look what he had in his hand." Br. Bede showed him the bomb.

A few men in the crowd began to approach in anger toward the monk who knocked-out one of their comrades. As the men got closer, they saw the size and menacing face of Br. Bede and backed off quickly. The crowd continued to swear and hurl insults at the four monks until the police arrived.

"Arrest that monk!" yelled someone in the crowd. "He just assaulted a man."

Br. Bede approached the officers with his hands out in a conciliatory gesture. "Yes, officer, I did hit the man," he said. "I hit him because he was about to throw *this* through the window of this bakery." He showed the officers the bomb and they immediately ordered everyone to back up lest the bomb detonate. Two of the officers dragged the limp Hunter Stephenson to safety by his arms as he was unable to move under his own power.

"Officer Banish," yelled the man in a captain's uniform. "Call for back-up, an ambulance and the bomb squad as quickly as you can."

Hunter was beginning to come around when he was startled by the appearance of several police officers and four black-robed monks. "Where am I?" he asked through a bloodied mouth.

"I think the better question," said the captain, as he pointed to the bomb, "is where were you going with that?"

"That's not mine," said Hunter. "I don't know what you are talking about."

"Sir," replied the officer, "we have at least eight witnesses who said that you were holding that thing before you got punched out."

"Well," he said, "that's just their word against mine. They could all be lying."

"But there are eight of them," countered the officer.

"OK," said Hunter, "then it's eight words against mine."

"Yeah right," said the cop as he led the now handcuffed Hunter into the back seat of a squad car.

Br. Bede shook his head and said, "Why in the world would he try something that stupid?"

Br. Philip responded, "Maybe he has an underdeveloped prefrontal cortex."

EPILOGUE

The next day, an article appeared in the *Detroit News* with the headline: **Monk KOs Punk Carrying Bomb.** Mrs. McNulty showed the article to Fr. Albert who posted it in the refectory for all to see. Br. Bede was embarrassed by the attention and felt that perhaps he deserved some humiliation for his actions. This, he thought, is not the kind of publicity the abbey needs. Then, a strange thing happened. Donations began to pour in to the abbey, from the general public. The gifts ranged from five dollars to one donation of ten thousand dollars. The money came in a steady stream for three or four weeks and in the end, totaled almost fifty thousand dollars. Most donations came with notes of support for Br. Bede and a general consensus that "It's about time!" It seemed, thought Fr. Albert, that he was not alone in lamenting the apparent demise of Judeo-Christian civilization.

Br. Canisius said a novena in gratitude for his recovered health and for the soul of Hunter Stephenson. All of the monks, in fact, prayed a great deal for Hunter. Forgiveness was second nature to them as they lived to emulate Christ. When asked how he could so easily forgive the man who almost killed, him he said, "If Christ can forgive a man like me, I can certainly return the favor to one whom Christ created.

Hunter Stephenson was tried and found guilty of attempting to bomb the Avalon Bakery. He was finally sentenced to real jail time for his actions. He was given ten years in the federal penitentiary at Milan, Michigan, during which time he was said to have converted to Christianity. Br. Bede welcomed the news but, always wary of jailhouse conversions, said, "Time will tell, but even in the twenty-first century, miracles happen every day."

Fr. Albert grew older with grace and with a new contentment about the world - and his place in it. He came to fully understand the meaning of being *in* the world without being *of* the world. This knowledge gave him a profound sense of peace. He began to gradually relinquish more of his daily responsibilities. As a result, Br. Bede assumed more duties each day, in preparation for his next role as abbot of St. Adelaide Abbey.

Br. Bede was ready. His spiritual growth over the years put him in the right place for a leadership role. He knew that when he wore the clothes of an abbot, he would be fair and kind to his brothers. He would encourage their development both as Christians and as men.

Br. Philp continued on his spiritual journey toward maturity. He still maintained a sense of humor which delighted his brothers, but he learned to be more prudent in its deployment. He, like Br. Bede, began to assume much more responsibility in the daily management of the abbey and was now considered to be a sub-prior – at such a young age. As his spirituality grew, his lust diminished accordingly. He maintained a written correspondence with Sarah Kessler who was now happily married and working at a local psychiatric hospital.

Br. Manuel soldiered on in the grand new kitchen which, he thought, seemed at odds with the neo-Gothic stonework edifice surrounding it. As he gazed upon the shiny stainless-steel appliances and sparkling white tile walls, he recalled what Br. Canisius had once said to Sarah Kessler: "We may be monks but we are not Amish." Always humble, Br. Manuel remained unmoved after his Bakewell tart recipe won the "Best Tart" category in a local newspaper's cooking contest. He had been surprised when Mrs. McNulty told him that she had secretly nominated him and that he had won. "That's fine," he said, "but I still find my sweet orange marmalade tart to be the best."

Br. Manuel's mention of orange marmalade enticed the angels to sing in his ear yet one more time.

ABOUT THE AUTHOR

Joe Mazzara is a retired Professor of Psychology and the author of the non-fiction books, *Pedal Cars & Purple Pickles* and *Liberty Ship Survivor: Why Ray Laenen is so Proud to be an American*. He has also been published in *Acoustic Guitar* magazine, *The Michigan Catholic* and dozens of other local publications. This is his first book of fiction. He lives in Clinton Township, Michigan with his wife, Cindy, and attends St. Peter Catholic Church in Mt. Clemens, Michigan.